The Dragon Chronicles:

The Unclaimed Beast

By

Dawn L. Lubertowicz

(Book 3)

Epilogue

Her heart sang to me every night since I was old enough to remember. As we got older, the scent rising off her skin made me itch to find her. I have not met her yet, but she haunts my dreams. I am certain that this girl, who rose up in my dreams like the fog on the mountains was meant to be my mate.

Every morning, I wake up realizing she isn't in my bed, I become depressed. I believe…no I am sure in my bones and soul that my time to find her is coming near. I will be twenty-five and the beast inside me couldn't wait to dig its fangs into her flesh and fly together as one in the sky. I need to claim her and forge our hearts together as one before she is lost to me forever.

I am her mate, as she is mine. We are alphas, meant to be together. I could sense she would be fierce like me, but that just thrilled my blood even more as the challenge was accepted.

Come, my darling, let our courtship begin…

Chapter One

"Place him here," an elderly woman ordered.

A couple of men carefully placed a young boy on a large, flat stone. The boy had his eyes screwed shut, letting out whimpers. Blood soaked cloths were pressed on his chest by a woman. She brushed his brown hair away from his face as she tried to hush him. His whimpers became louder, but he remained brave and only cried softly, even though he should be screaming in pain. The elderly woman knew she needed to tear her eyes away from him before he ended up bleeding to death. Looking around the cave, she hoped the person she was looking for was here.

"Amara!" the female elder called out.

The other adults scanned the cave, the color draining from their faces. They feared the rumbling that just happened may be an earthquake. Without a warning, a huge shadowy figure appeared in front of them. They all took a few steps back, except for the older woman, as their eyes became wide as saucers. The figure slowly shifted and twisted until it became a smaller one. Some let out gasps as they saw a naked female slowly walked out from the shadows and stood before the elderly woman.

"Madelyn, it has been too long," the mysterious woman spoke softly.

"It has, Amara," Madelyn said.

Amara looked around the cave at the other humans. They couldn't take their eyes from her. Amara gently shook her head to let her red hair shimmer in the light from the torches; the locks looked as though they were on fire. She wasn't expecting company, or else she would had prepared a meal for them and maybe dressed in some type of clothing so they wouldn't gawk at her flesh. Looking back at Madelyn, her red eyes glowed in the lightly dim cave.

"So what brings you here, old friend?" Amara questioned.

Madelyn quickly turned and left Amara to rush to the young boy on the stone table. Looking back, she saw Amara was still confused by her surprised visit.

"It's my grandson, Gordon," she replied. She swallowed before continuing. "He fell onto debris and punctured his chest. Please, he's in

4

need of your help. I'm afraid he has damaged his heart," Madelyn begged, tears in her eyes.

Amara slowly moved toward the boy, causing some of the humans to back away. She could tell they were afraid of her; she flowed along the ground like something supernatural. She smirked; they should have known they were dealing with a dragon. They were lucky she didn't come out into the light in her dragon form, as that probably would have scared them away, especially the boy's mother.

Once close to the boy, she watched as his flesh became pale. Soft whimpers continued to come out of his mouth between pants and sweat slowly slid across his skin. Looking at the bandages on his chest, her hand slowly reached out to them. She drew it back when it was almost slapped. Amara quickly glared at the woman she guessed was the boy's mother when her body almost reacted to keep her son safe. The woman lowered her eyes as Amara looked at the bandages again. Slowly removing the cloths, she heard a wet stickiness to it. She kept her composure so they wouldn't know how serious the boy's injuries were. Staring at the hole in his chest, she saw he would be dead in an hour or two if they moved him again.

Glancing over at Madelyn, she saw on her face that she knew the answer. Amara looked at the boy, as he didn't seem to cry out too much. She hid a smile, knowing he was very brave considering his severe injuries. If it was anyone else, they would be a hollering and twisting around, worsening the wound.

She would have to admit the boy was different. He kept his composure and tried to hide how much pain he was in. He seemed to be concerned with making the others worry about him so he did his best to keep quiet. That quality made her aware that he was meant for something great.

She made up her mind and knew how she was going to save the boy. Looking over at Madelyn when her lotus flower diamond ring caught her attention, the purple diamond petals had glimmered in light and always had her staring at it since she was young. It was a present from Madelyn's husband, the mineral so striking it caught the eye of many dragons in her family. She didn't know what it was, but it was as if it put them in a trance when it glimmered.

Shaking off the trance to look at the aging friend of her family, Amara had to help. Madelyn and her family had always been friends with her kind so when she asked for a favor, Amara would never turn her away. Madelyn's family were gypsies, but always respected the dragons' way without questioning. That was why Madelyn's family was allowed to stay at a location that Amara's family had always protected. It held special minerals that could be shaped into metal that could easily slice through others scales, but Amara's kind were immune to it for some reason. Amara's tribe had trusted that Madelyn's kind would never harm them so they had nothing to worry about.

Looking back at the boy they called Gordon, she knew he was destined for something great. Without much thought, she knew how she would save him.

"I'll help him," Amara said softly with a smile.

Before they could stop her, she sliced open her chest. She laughed to herself as the humans cringed when they heard her cracking through her ribs. Her claws dug deeply into the one muscle she was searching for. Her heart skipped a beat as she tore a part of it away. Looking into her bloody hand, she watched the small part of her heart beat. Everyone moved away from as Amara leaned in to see where she could place the piece of her heart so Gordon would have a chance to live. As she placed it into

Gordon, a light shone brightly and quickly. Another smile spread on her face as she saw her the piece of her organ merging with Gordon's damaged heart. Looking into his face, his eyes locked with hers. She saw he was going to be okay. He couldn't speak loudly, but she caught it perfectly with her superior hearing.

"Thank you," he whispered.

Amara moved away from Gordon as his parents swept in to look him over. They were filled with joy, though still afraid to move him too much. She knew he would be fine as the new piece of heart was already healing his wound and pumping her blood through him. She stopped and looked over at Madelyn.

"Be warned, he might not be like his kind anymore. He might be more resilient to injuries and illnesses than any mortal," Amara warned.

"I understand," Madelyn said before bowing her head. "Thank you so much for saving my grandson." There were tears of joy in her eyes.

Placing a hand on Madelyn's shoulder, she raised her head. "I just hoped he uses his new found life wisely."

"I'll make sure he does," the old woman promised.

"Good," Amara said softly.

Madelyn went over to be with her grandson. Amara watched as the mortals seemed very pleased that the young boy would live. Her smile slowly disappeared, as she had been alone for a long time and hadn't seen any of her kind. She was left there to protect the area from being tainted by men who would do more harm than good. Her family stretched out to other areas to protect, but to her knowledge they met their fate at the hands of dragon hunters. She looked up to the sky and let out mournful howl to see if any of her kind would come to her, but no one answered. She started to believe she was the last of her kind.

That idea, of course, had not detoured her of her sworn duty. Many men had come to try to enter the woods, but she had them running for their lives. The only ones she allowed close to her were Madelyn's family because she knew they could be trusted. Madelyn made sure they followed the oath of do no harm to her kind.

As Madelyn and her family left, Amara's heart became cold and dark. She wrapped her arms around her, feeling more alone than before. It was a sweet moment to have company, but when they left it always reminded her that she didn't belong with their group and she may never see another one of her kind.

Closing her eyes, she thought maybe she could recall her dreams from all the times she had fallen asleep. She felt like she was in the same room with another of her kind. Her heart skipped a beat, thinking it may be true. They used to share long conversations until the sun rose and she would wake up from it. The smile returned to her face, hoping that maybe someday she could find this other dragon so she wouldn't be alone any longer.

Her happy thought was interrupted when a twinge shot through her mind. Letting out a growl, she knew her hope would have to wait as she felt a few mortals entering the area. Digging her claws into the cave's wall, she climbed up to an opening. She leaned out from the outside with her one set of claws dug into it. Looking out into the distance, she sniffed the air a few times before knowing where those mortals were. She leapt off the wall and quickly turned into her dragon's form. Letting out a roar, she hoped this would scare them before she showed up.

***

Liam's head sprung up as a wicked smile crossed his face. He had been waiting to feel something from the mysterious female dragon that haunted his dreams. Leaping onto the windowsill of his castle, he sniffed the air. He squinted to see as far as his precise vision could see. Knowing where he was going, he jumpstarted from the windowsill and transformed into his dragon form. His wings flapped quickly into the unyielding wind. He wanted to reach the female dragon before she faced the danger she was getting herself into. He just hoped the headwind wouldn't slow him down.

Looking at the earth below him, he spotted a group of men surrounding a human female. He sniffed the air and knew instantly it was the mysterious female dragon, but for some odd reason she wore a human form. He let out a bellowing roar, causing the men to look up. Baring his razor sharped talons and teeth, he forced them back. He saw an opening to save the girl and spun his body in the air as it twisted and turned into his human form. The girl was under him as he stood up straight. He looked around him to see if the men would do anything. Growling, he wanted to make sure they stayed where they were.

Ignoring the woman, he felt her glare burning a hole right through him, but he didn't care. He needed to get her out of here before those men resumed back to the trap. In an instant, Liam spun again and changed into his dragon form. He let out a big roar, shaking the ground beneath his claws. Before the men could charge at him with their weapons, he picked up the woman and took off at high speed. The wind threw dirt to make the men cover their eyes.

Once reaching above the clouds, Liam soared through them. He let out a raspy laugh as the female tried with all her might to get out of his talons. He was not about to lose her. All the times she visited in his dreams, he had tried to track her down or coax her to stay with him, but she always faded away like the morning fog when the sun rose.

If he were in his human form, her biting might have caused him to flinch, but he knew his scales kept him safe. Taking a quick peek at her when she stopped struggling, he wondered why she hadn't changed back into her dragon form. He became worried that maybe she couldn't change. In his dreams, she was always human, so he wasn't sure if she could change. Sniffing the air, he could tell that he picked up the right girl, but hoped she hadn't lost her ancestry form.

Tucking his wings against his body, he soared down quickly. As the clouds revealed the ground below, he spotted his castle. His wings spread again to slow them down so they could descend gently. Flapping, he gradually dropped the girl on the ground. Her red eyes burned bright as two hot coals. He almost winced from her gazed, but ignored her. He could tell she wasn't happy about the situation. His feet touched the ground softly only a few feet away from her. Turning around, he saw her slowly getting on her hands and knees. He tilted his head to the side, wondering what she was doing. Without warning, she turned into a red-scaled beast and let out a roar. Smiling, he was glad she hadn't lost her ability to change. Her talons dug deep into the ground before she propelled herself toward him. He just stood his ground, knowing she wouldn't hurt him.

She went down like a ton of bricks when his furry beasts jumped on her. One slammed her head on the ground as she snorted in irritation. A second one approached, inspecting the metallic probes against her neck with both of its heads. Electricity surge through her body before she finally gave up.

As Liam walked toward her, he changed back into his human form as she did too. Crouching down, he couldn't wipe the big ass smile from his face. His minions got off of her as she changed back and one placed a silver collar on her with a purple gem in the middle that glowed when he closed it around her neck. The others placed similar items on her wrists and ankles. Each purple gem glowed to show it was secure. The leader of the beasts walked over and threw her over its shoulder.

As Liam moved closer, another minion handed him a silver bracelet with a red gem. It glowed once he sealed it around his right wrist. He slowly examined the girl, wondering where she had been hiding all that time. Wasn't she ever lonely? Hadn't she ever ventured out from the area she hid in? Shaking his head to get focus of what he needed to do next, he knew it was going to take some time to get her acquainted with him.

"Let's go," he ordered.

Leading the beasts back into the castle, Liam wondered if it would be possible to share a life like the one he had in his dreams with her. He hoped so, because he thought he was the last of his kind until the dreams started and he soon realized that there was another out there, somewhere. He just hoped she would accept him so maybe they would at least have each other.

Chapter Two

Amara stirred, touching her head and letting out a groan when she felt the ache in her head. Her eyes quickly widened when she realized she wasn't in her forest any more. Looking around wildly, getting on her hands and knees, she tried to change into her dragon form to escape the tower. Grinding her teeth, she struggled to change, but nothing seemed to work. She let out an irritated yell before her eyes went to a steel door. Growling at the figure that came in, she had no idea what happened, but she wasn't going down without a fight. Even if the figure was a handsome, bearded male dragon.

***

Liam hadn't been able to stop smiling, even when facing someone who wanted to kill him. He saw so much hatred in those ruby-colored eyes of hers, but he could stare into them for an eternity. He finally looked away from her gaze as he examined the rest of her. He wouldn't mind seeing her porcelain-colored skin, but he decided it would be best to have her dressed so she wouldn't be any angrier with him than she already was.

"What do you want?" she growled.

He looked at her face and saw how twisted it was as she bared her teeth, a growl escaping her. He was actually lost for words when he finally got to see her in person. He had rehearsed their meeting so many times but his well-practiced words were gone as the jitters got worse. Placing a hand on his stomach, he felt the butterflies fluttering faster and faster, making his insides twist and turn. He couldn't believe he reacted to her like that, as he thought for sure he was well prepared for her arrival. Another growl escaped her, drawing him back from his thoughts.

"I have brought you here to claim you," he said.

Liam didn't realize those words came out of his mouth. That wasn't what he wanted to say. She lowered her body like a cat ready to pounce.

"The hell you are!"

Liam worried he made a mistake, as she didn't seem like the same woman in his dreams. There they would sit and talk like there was no tomorrow, but the woman before him seemed angry, as though she hated him. She didn't seem like she wanted to chit-chat about the weather. She looked around wildly and then screwed her eyes shut. He soon realized what she was trying to do, but knew it wouldn't happen. She opened her eyes when she realized the same thing.

"Why can't I change?"

"Because of the brand spanking new jewelry you're wearing." He gestured toward her left wrist.

She quickly lifted one wrist, then the other as she leaned back on her legs. Her hand swiftly touched her neck and felt another metal object around it. Her eyes burned brighter, letting out low, rattling growls.

"Uh-uh, be nice," Liam ordered.

Her eyes' brightness slowly faded as confusion flooded them, furrowing her brow. He lifted up his right arm, showing with his left hand.

"See this, I can do whatever I want to you," he explained.

She crawled on the bed until her back hit the stone wall. He realized quickly that the hunter had become the prey. Fisting his right hand, her wrists clanked together. Her eyes widened as she struggled against the pull. Gradually, she floated off the bed toward him. Her arms, still together, above her head, she came face to face with him.

"With these fancy trinkets, I'm able to make you do whatever I want," he explained before leaning in.

Amara turned her face away from him and closed her eyes. "Please, don't," she begged with a shaky voice.

Liam slowly leaned back and his eyes searched her. He felt bad for making her tremble with fear, as he wasn't planning to do anything. He just wanted her companionship, and he'd acted like a monster ready to take her flesh. His fingers brushed through the air to let her float back onto the bed and gently bounce on it when the bracelets weren't holding her up anymore.

***

Amara watched with curiosity as he swiftly left her. She wasn't sure what was going on, but really thought he was going to force himself on her. He did a complete one eighty, confusing her even more. She stared down at her wrists and didn't know how she was going to get out of this. As her eyes searched the room, they landed on the only window, but it was high up.

Jumping off the bed, she quickly went to the wall and looked up. It looked as if she would have to climb to get to it, but maybe it may be a way out. Finding cracks in the wall, she began her slow climb. Hopping onto the stone windowsill, her hope and happiness went away. The window would only provide light from the sun, but there was no way for her escape. Wrapping her fingers around the steel bars, she knew they wouldn't be ones she could easily break, as some of her strength was hindered.

Resting her back against the stone frame, she just stared out into the distance, wondering if her land was okay without her. Pulling her knees toward her chest and wrapping her arms around them, she laid the side of her face on them, feeling the sadness engulfing her heart. She didn't know how she was going to get back to her family's land. Her body shook from all the bad thoughts of how those mortal men were going to go back to where they were hired and informed the village she was gone. Then they would come in and destroy the land by chopping down all the ancient trees and killing every single critter, big or small.

Letting out a soft growl, she knew those men were hunters, but it was too late when she was about to attack them. They had sent up an electrical, pulsating chain net that had weakened her and caused her to change back to her human form. As those hunters surrounded her, she was trying to heal from her injuries from the fall. Before she knew it, she felt another presence. She looked up and saw a silver scaled dragon flying down before changing into its human form. She was shocked to see another dragon, let alone a male. Amara didn't have a chance to say anything before he decided to kidnap her. She would have done a better job of getting away if she wasn't already weakened by the hunters' trap.

Once she felt the ground under her, her strength returned, and she was planning to attack the male, but once again she was subdued. She hated that her day wasn't turning out to be routine. Her mind started to wander, thinking that maybe she was weakened easily because she gave that boy part of her heart. She shook her head to get rid of such a thought. It was a minute part of her that shouldn't matter.

Amara continued to stare out into the distance as the sun began to set. A silver tear slowly made its way off her face and hit the stone floor below. She ran through some ideas she had on how to escape. The first step was to remove those damn shackles so he couldn't control her anymore. Her body trembled at the thought of what he might do to her.

Closing her eyes, she tried to go back to her happy memories where she didn't fear such things.

***

"And that's how I broke my arm when I climbed that damn tree…"

Amara slowly opened her eyes as the chuckle from a boy telling her a childhood story echoed through her mind. Stretching, she wasn't shocked to discover she was still a prisoner. She was hoping that she was somewhere else, like in the dream. Pulling her knees against her again, she looked out the window, thinking about those dreams.

She didn't know why they flowed through her mind, but there was always someone else there, a boy or actually nowadays it had been a man. She could never see him, but knew he was in the same room with her. There was never a quiet moment in this dark room as they would talk on and on like they had known each other their whole lives. Of course, when she woke up, she would feel even more alone. There were times where she was tempted to stay with him as he would try to coax her to stay, but as the sun rose, she always woke up. She didn't really have a choice as the sun seemed to break the spell of the dream had on her. Continuing to watch the sun rise, she let out a sad sigh, wishing to be back home.

***

A man chopped away at a tree as the others were carrying wood away. They stilled when they heard something. They weren't sure they heard correctly, as those hunters told them the dragon that guarded the area was gone. Before they knew it, a roar echoed above them. Running from the flames that spewed down from above, the men yelled, trying to avoid getting burned.

A huge creature landed on the ground with a heavy thud. Looking around, he thought it sensed and heard a howl from a female dragon here. He moved around as his black and red scales glimmered in the morning sun. He really thought he may have a chance with a female, but she didn't seem to be here. Sniffing the air, he let out a growl. Apparently, she was taken by another male dragon. Roaring, he took off into the sky to try to locate her again before the other male got to her first. He had travelled too far to lose her again.

***

Liam continued on his way to Amara's room. He woke up from the dream where he was telling her how he broke his arm when he was younger. Letting out a sigh, he wished they could communicate like that now, but he knew she hated him for some reason. Didn't she realize that they must have been meant to be? When he saw her the first time outside the dream, she didn't seem to recognize him. In the dream, they were inseparable, but outside she acted as if he was the enemy and wanted nothing to do with him. He knew it was her by what he saw in the dream. Most of the time, they were sitting in a dark room talking. He imagined them lying in bed, telling each other their stories, hopes and dreams.

Reaching her door, he stared at it, wondering if last night's dream changed something and she was ready to be herself with him. He pulled the skeleton key out of his pocket. His hands were sweaty from nerves and that fact that he'd kept them in his pockets the whole walk. Going through each key slowly, he hoped she would be the girl he met in his dreams. He would have the right key if his hands hadn't shaken so much, but he kept dropping them. Exhaling sharply, he hated how nervous he was around her. It shouldn't be that way, as they'd grown up together, even if it was only in his dreams.

Before he was around the door, something went whooshing passed his head. Looking over his shoulder, he saw Amara standing there, panting with so much anger and hatred on her face that her features twisted in disgust. He quickly shut and locked the door so he could turn to face her. He watched her carefully to see if she would throw anything else at him. He still couldn't wrap his head around her. She was the complete opposite of what she was in his dreams. He began to second guess himself and believed he picked up the wrong girl.

"What is wrong with you?" he yelled before he could stop himself from losing his temper.

Liam didn't know why he was being like that with her, but she had him all twisted up inside. He wanted to grab her by the shoulders and shake out the girl he thought he knew. He ducked when she threw a vase filled with flowers. He heard it crash behind him before he slowly stood up. Now, she was in a stare off with him. He wanted to flinch so much from her glare, but he stood his ground.

***

Amara continued to glare at the male dragon in his human form as she felt so much anger and hatred for him for bringing her there and taking her away from her home. But in her heart, it fluttered, especially when he spoke. It was like it was trying to tell her that she knew the man before her, but she didn't believe she did.

She looked around the room for something else to throw at him so maybe he would leave her alone to plan out her escape. All she had left was her pillow. Picking that up, she quickly tossed it at him. He arched his brow, not believing she threw something as soft and feathery as a pillow. She knew it was a stupid idea, but it was all she had left to try to make him leave. She snarled at him, hoping to make him go away. She soon realized this was a mistake when his emerald green eyes shifted from shock to anger. She backed up until she felt the bed on the back of her legs. Amara had forgotten that he could easily make her do whatever he wanted with the stupid contraptions on her. She begged a million times in her head that he wouldn't and would have apologized if her vocal cords hadn't decided to stop working. His demeanor changed, making her believed he heard her silent plead.

"Are you hungry?" he asked softly.

Amara would have declined such an invitation, but she was hungry, plus just the way he looked at her made her believe something else. Maybe he was actually a nice guy. She threw that theory out, knowing she should just go along with him as he could use the gems to control her. Lowering her head, she gave him the illusion she had given in.

"Yes," she answered quietly.

***

Liam was glad things were starting to go this way. He thought for sure he would have to drag her to breakfast kicking and screaming. His body began to relax, glad he didn't have to keep fighting with her. He didn't understand why she resisted him on everything when in his dreams she was agreeable with a lot of things.

Who is this girl?

***

As they walked to the kitchen, Liam tried to get her to talk, but she kept her head down and acted submissive. He began to wonder again if she was the wrong girl, because she was nothing like the one in his dreams. Wondering what he could to do break her out of her shell, he spotted an interesting piece. He stopped and gently grabbed her arm to turn her toward the tapestries that were hanging.

"These have been in my family for a long time," he said, removing his hand from her arm.

"Oh," was all she said.

He tried to think of other ways to get her interested in having a conversation. He rubbed the material between his fingers.

"These were made with the finest materials," he continued.

"I see."

"Yep, it took my ancestors a long time to make."

"How interesting."

Liam let out an irritated sigh. He was hoping for more insight instead of simple answers. He was about to say something to her to try and snap her out of that strange behavior, but when he turned his head, he found an empty space next to him. Looking toward a doorway, he felt where she had gone.

***

Amara took the opportunity of the male being preoccupied with the tapestries. He didn't realize she slowly slid away from him as she gave him simple answers to distract him. She ran across the stone bridge, hoping to get somewhere he wouldn't find her until she could figure out how to remove the damn silver shackles.

Her heart skipped a beat when she thought she was close to freedom. She quickly inhaled the fresh air as she ran, listening as her feet padded against the hard, cold bridge. Good thing her soles were accustomed to such conditions or else it would be harder for her to run away.

Before she was halfway across it, big creatures climbed up the sides and stood in her way. She slid to a stop as someone climbed down the biggest creature with a smirk on his face.

"Where do you think you're going?" he gloated.

She would love to slap that smirk off his face, but she realized she probably wouldn't be able to do so with all his furry friends around. She took a few steps back when he walked toward her with his hand out.

"Now, are you going to go back with me or do we need to do this the hard way?" he asked.

Looking around, she saw her chances. Even a quick peek behind those monsters, she could see her freedom not too far.

"Well?"

She glared at him when he brought her back from her thought of freedom by speaking. She made a decision as she calculated her chances. She quickly crossed her arms and legs before plopping down on the ground. She would have cried out from the sudden pain from sitting too quickly on the stone ground, but she was determined to make him work at this.

"Alright, let's do it the hard way," he said with a big grin.

Amara tightened her arms against her, showing she was ready to fight. This just made him smile bigger. She furrowed her brow, squinting her eyes to dare him to do his worst. He mirrored her facial expression, crossing his arms as well. She wasn't impressed that they were back into their staring contest again, but she wasn't going to back down now. She was so close to freedom. If she could just find an opening, then she would be free and away from him.

Bring it on, Mr. Big Ego!

***

It took a while, but Liam was able to pry Amara's nails off the doorway. He had thrown her over his shoulder as she began her tantrum. She had tried to punch and kick him, but he wasn't affected by it as he attempted to piss her off more by smacking her ass. That really caused her internal inferno to flare up to its highest intensity. He almost wasn't able to hold onto her as she became a feral cat about to be put in a bathtub full of water. He didn't know why he liked pissing her off, but he began to enjoy the challenge.

Liam felt the stings of her claws cutting him, but he knew they wouldn't last long. Just like the lacerations, he knew the bruises would go away thanks to his healing powers. He tried his best not to hurt her too much as her powers were hindered by the gems. Purposely bumping into furniture and walls, he knew this would rattle her up again when she tired from her tantrum. He just needed her to keep it up, as it seemed to feed the need that lay inside of him in a dormant state.

Liam pushed opened a door with his hand and then smacked her butt again. He chuckled as she started kicking, yelling, and punching again. His pants tightened from her fighting spirit, but he ignored it as he threw her down. She was about to attack him, but soon realized she was on a bed. He let a wicked smile slide across his face; he was going to enjoy this. Her eyes returned to his and he could see the fear behind them.

Moving his right hand, she laid on her back. Fisting his right hand, her wrists clasped together. The wicked smile grew into a twisted, evil grin as her eyes begged him not to. In another swift movement of his hand, her legs spread opened. Her body trembled in front of him as his eyes examined her from head to toe. He wanted to bury himself inside her, but he didn't want to do it on those terms. Looking back into her eyes, he saw the fear increased as tears flowed down her face.

"Please, don't," she begged in a shaky voice.

He felt his heart plummet at her words. He wasn't going to do anything against her will, he was just trying to get her to challenge him more, but all he did was cause her fear and probably made her believe he was nothing more than a monster. Closing his eyes, lowering his head, he realized he took things too far. Clenching his right hand again, she was released from the power of the gems. She curled up into a ball and cried uncontrollably. He couldn't watch anymore and decided he should just leave.

***

Amara looked up when she heard the steel door shutting. The click of the lock confirmed her thought she was a prisoner. Curling tighter into a ball, she tried to keep her body from trembling so badly, but she knew how close he came taking her. She would have fought, but she choked and froze. She couldn't really move as so many terrible thoughts rushed through her mind. Luckily, he didn't take her flesh and for some reason, he released her from her position. At least, she was alone…for the moment. Calming her breathing, she tried to focus on her plan of escape.

Chapter Three

Liam didn't like how things ended between him and the woman. He decided to check on her while bringing something to eat. After unlocking the door, he softly knocked to let her know he was coming in. He quickly looked around to find her before she tried to escape again. Quietly walking in, he gently placed the tray of food on a small, wooden table as his eyes couldn't seem to move away from what he saw. On the windowsill was the female with her knees up against her chest and her arms wrapped around them lazily. Her eyes were closed and she breathed softly, the side of her face on her knees.

Swallowing hard, he loved seeing her relaxed as he moved toward her. Sitting across from her, he continued to watch her sleep. It would be the first time since he brought her to his home that she wasn't fighting with him and trying to get away. He was going to take this chance so he could admire her better. Her radiant auburn hair glowed like embers from the afternoon sun.

Leaning forward, he gently brushed some of her hair behind her ear. He made sure to be careful so he wouldn't wake her up. He wanted to enjoy that moment a little bit longer before she went back to the wicked wench that caused such distress in him. He finally got his entrails all untangled from their earlier fight. Leaning back against the wooden frame, he stared out into the distance, releasing a contented sigh. His mind whirled around, trying to figure out how he was going to get her to be the girl he knew from the dreams.

***

Liam allowed Amara out of the room when it was dinner time. He was hoping that would be a better situation, but he was wrong. She kept her eyes lowered and softly sipped the soup in front of her. He could tell she was nervous by the way she jumped every time there was a noise. He didn't want to be like that' he wished they could be like the couple he recalled from the dreams.

Why is she acting like this?

After staring at her for a while at the other end of the long table, he looked down at the opened book in front of him. He didn't know how to make small talk in the real world so he had been reading the same page over and over again. Trying not to appear nervous as well, he sneakily wiped his sweaty hands.

***

Sipping on her soup quietly, Amara took a quick peek at her dinner host. His black hair glimmered in the light as if it was a smooth silk dress. Every once in a while, he would bring the spoon to his mouth and then put it back in the bowl after he ate some of it. She hid her giggle with her hand when there was a dribble of soup in his beard. Her eyes flowed down to his other hand lying on the book to keep it open. Either he was a slow reader or he wasn't reading at all; he hadn't turned the page yet. She eyed him suspiciously, wondering why he had chosen her. Could it be true that maybe they were the last of their kind or was it something else? Admiring him more, she figured it had nothing to do with love.

It's a shame he's a dragonknapper…he's pretty attractive.

Continuing to eat her soup, she shouldn't prey on such an idea of love seeing he was nothing more than an evil prison warden, wanting only one thing from her. She came to the conclusion that he found out she may be the last female dragon around so he had to take the opportunity to snatch her up in case there were other males out there.

Her heart fluttered when she went back to when she woke up that evening. She was still on the windowsill in the room he locked her in as she felt another presence in the room. When she looked up, she saw emerald green eyes just staring at her. Not in a lustful, creepy way, but in admiration. As their eyes locked, she had to force herself to look away as she didn't like sensing the feeling inside of her. She pretended to watch the sun set and hoped he would do the same, but she felt his eyes were still on her. Daring to look back into those soft green eyes, she hoped he would feel awkward and look away, but he didn't. She was now locked with his eyes and didn't want to look away. Finally, he made the first move.

"Are you hungry?" he asked softly.

"Yes."

"Okay." He cleared his throat.

Standing up first, he held out his hand for her to grab. She eyed him suspiciously, not knowing where it was going. After a while, she finally grabbed hold of it and helped her to her feet. As she ripped her hand out of his, she clumsily fell forward. Slowly looking up, her body began to tremble again, but for a different reason. Her hands pressed against his chest, his arms wrapped around her to keep her standing up. Once her mind began to think, she pushed him away from her. Her heart was okay with being like that with him, but she knew she shouldn't get too cozy with him; she still needed to escape.

Peeking over, brushing hair behind her ear, she saw a hurt look on his face, but soon it disappeared to an emotionless stare. She pretended to look around the room to avoid getting locked with his eyes, again. She needed to stop feeling like that or else she might not want to leave.

She returned from the memory when she heard someone clear their throat. Looking up, she caught him staring at her again. Shaking her head to get out of his spell, she quickly rearranged the silverware on the table.

"Um, I'm sorry?"

"I said, we should get to know each other," he replied sternly.

"Why does it matter who I am?"

He flinched as if she slapped him across the face. She didn't know why she was fired up again, but it may be that he sounded arrogant or because she was being held against her will. She glared at him again, knowing that her red eyes burned like hot coals. She thought he would melt away from her glare, but he seemed stubborn.

"I just figured we could act civilized, but apparently you don't want to," he grated.

"Oh, I'm sorry, you don't want to play caveman that dragged me by the hair, anymore?" she hissed, crossing her arms.

"Are you suggesting I have a one track mind?"

"No, I'm calling you a big dumb blockhead!"

"I saved your life!"

"I had everything under control!"

"Not from where I was standing."

"Ha! Obviously, you didn't look at the whole picture. As a typical male you were probably staring at my breasts!" she yelled, squeezing her breasts with her crossed arms.

"I saw you were in danger."

"Like I said, I was fine. I'm not a damsel in distress that needed rescuing!"

"Oh, yeah, you had it all under control when you were lying on the ground!"

***

Her eyes burned so bright that he was almost terrified of her.

Almost.

Covering his face with his hand and letting out a sigh, he was annoyed by how much she wanted to fight with him. He was half tempted to let her go… well, almost. Uncovering his face, he looked at her again. He was hoping she would have calmed down a little bit during that time, but he realized she was still up in arms and kept her defenses up as well. Tapping his finger on the wooden table, it echoed in the awkward silence. Her saucy attitude caused his eye to twitch a few times before he rubbed it to stop. He decided he was going to try one more time to get where they were in his dreams.

"Can we please try to be civil?" he asked harshly.

He didn't mean it to come out like it did, but it was already out. He was just hoping for some conversation instead of silence. He had dealt with the silence when he was living there alone. Liam hoped that maybe she would brighten up his days with some meaningful conversation. She looked like she was about to start spewing out more harmful things and he didn't want to hear it.

"Please?" he begged softly.

She softened a little. She still had her arms crossed, but at least some of her walls were crumbling a little. Feeling the throbbing pain in his stomach, he knew it was the result of her. There was some fluttering when he realized he would have to start the conversation. He didn't know why he felt so nervous around her as he had many conversations with her before… well in his dreams.

"So, what's your name?"

"Amara," she answered emotionless.

Flinching, he felt the sting from her answer. He knew it would take a while before they could have a normal conversation. He continued to stare at her, hoping she would take a hint to keep the conversation going. She rolled her eyes, letting out a heavy sigh.

"What's your name, caveman?"

Shaking his head, he couldn't believe how things were going. He hoped she would let her walls down so maybe they could get to know each other better in the real world than in their dreams. Both his index fingers slowly rose before falling and hitting the table.

"Liam," he answered with disbelief in his voice.

"Uh, I figure it would have been: me, Atouck, you, girl I hit over head with club," she mocked.

He raised his eyebrow. "Seriously? You're going to be like this?"

She mirrored his raised eyebrow. "Seriously? You're going to be like this?"

"Come on!" he yelled after slamming his palms down.

She made a few grunting noises. "Sorry, I don't speak caveman."

Even though he didn't want to, he glared into her eyes as they sat there in complete silence. Things certainly weren't going as planned.

41

Eventually, he looked away, crossing his arms. He began to believe he'd made a mistake. He should have known those dreams were nothing real; he was only fooling himself, believing she was the one for him.

Pushing up his sleeve, he scratched his forearm. The only thing that brought him out of his angry thoughts was a gasp. Looking over, he saw her eyes were widen, no hatred as the anger left them. He wondered what she was shocked about and soon realized she was looking at his scar on his forearm.

"What are you looking at?" he asked.

"That scar," she said.

"What about it?"

Shaking her head, she lowered her gaze toward her lap. "Never mind, it's nothing."

Liam arched his eyebrow. He knew she was hiding something, but for some reason she wouldn't say. He crossed his arms again, covering the scar. Listening to the grandfather clock ticked away, he waited to see if she would say anything or if they would return to silence. He was hoping she would at least talk about something, anything. He expected her to run willingly into his arms, to gush with excitement as she voiced secrets and joys they'd only ever discussed in their dreams. Instead, she spewed venom with every word, the fiery cut of her glare slicing through his every hope until he realized there was no hope at all. She was not the same at all.

Later, while waiting for her to start the conversation again, he noticed her nodding off. He eventually gave up on any talking tonight. He made sure to stay close to her as he walked her back to the tower room. He didn't want to take a chance of her escaping, as he might try fresh tomorrow. Maybe today was just a bad day, hopefully tomorrow would be better.

***

Amara kept her eyes lowered as they walked toward her room. She kept biting her lower lip and felt it becoming cracked and chapped. She wanted to ask about his scar, but she didn't want to believe that something could be true. Peeking over at him, she saw he was deep in thought as well. She looked over at his covered arm, wishing she could see it again to make sure she saw it correctly before confirming her thoughts. Quickly looking up at his face, she studied him for a while, wondering what he was up to. She figured he would have already taken her flesh, but he seemed to be trying to be a gentleman in all of this. Laughing to herself, she must have gone insane to believe that. He had kidnapped her and brought her there like a prisoner. That wasn't what gentlemen did.

Did they?

She was too focused on him that she missed the floor carpet being ruffled up. She put her hands out to try to catch herself, but realized she wasn't falling anymore. Looking up, she stared right into his eyes. She couldn't seem to move, their gazes locked as she found herself lost in his emerald eyes. She placed her hand on his face and felt how soft his beard. Before she could do anything, he pulled her tighter against him and placed his mouth over hers. Heat surged through her in an instant. She wanted to fight him off her, but her body molded against his. She relaxed and let him kiss her. Letting all his feelings rush through her, tears threatened to fall. She had never felt like that before, where someone needed her so much that caused them pain.

Amara didn't want to, but she had to push him away before the pain got worse. Panting, her body shook from the sudden temperature change. She had to focus, looking at the floor to keep from looking him in his eyes. She knew what she would see if she did and she didn't want him to see right through her defenses. She needed to stay strong so she wouldn't lose herself to playing the role of damsel in distress. She had always been alone and able to take care of herself. She didn't need some caveman to pretend to be a knight in shining armor to rescue her. Placing her hand on her stomach, she could felt the contents ready to come out. She closed her eyes to calm herself so that wouldn't happen. Feeling him moving, she put a hand out to keep him back.

"Please, take me back to my room," she begged with a shaky voice.

She thought for sure he would fight with her about the stupid thing that just happened, but was glad when he didn't say anything and turned to walk. She stayed behind him so he wouldn't see her wiping away her silver tears. She didn't need someone worrying about her. She would be perfectly fine in a matter of minutes. She was capable of taking care of herself.

***

Liam didn't want to take her back the tower. He wanted to explore the kiss they shared more deeply, but he knew she would end up shutting down if he pushed any harder. Opening the door for her, she quickly went in. He spotted silver tears on her face and would have asked if she was okay, but he knew she would just fight him about it. He let it go as she reached the middle of the room. He slowly shut the door, staring at her before he couldn't see her anymore. Locking her inside, he knew that wasn't right either, but he didn't want to chance the possibility of her escaping.

Leaning his forehead against the cold stone, it was hardly enough to temper the fire of his longing for her. All he wanted was his perfect companion from his dreams and wondered if she was just pretended to be this way so she can get out of their relationship. He so much wanted to go in there and shake the truth out of her so he wasn't wasting his time with something that wasn't there. But he knew he couldn't let her go, he had put in so much into the relationship that he knew it would be too painful. She wasn't like other females. For some reason, she had to prove she was tough even though there were times she didn't need to be. Letting out a sigh, he figured he should get some rest.

Maybe tomorrow would be better. Of course, he had a feeling that rest wouldn't be easy tonight.

What a girl…

***

"Can I see your arm?" a female voice asked.

"Sure, can I ask what for?" a male voice questioned

"I just wanted to check something."

"Satisfied?"

"Yeah, exactly what I thought."

The male let out a chuckle. "You're a weird one."

"Well, it takes one to know one," she teased.

They both laughed as it echoed in the lightly dim room. The female only saw the male's arm in a small amount of light that seemed to spotlight what she was looking for. She began to feel like she was being pulled back. She knew what it meant as she closed her eyes. She wanted to stay longer, but she knew she couldn't.

***

Amara slowly opened her eyes. She knew she couldn't stay with the male too long as the sun seemed to be the beacon that called her back to reality. Sitting up slowly, she noticed she was still in the tower room. She hoped maybe that was all a dream, but it seemed like she was still a prisoner. Looking down at her left wrist, she tried to push the silver band off, but she knew it wouldn't happen.

She moved toward the edge of the bed and gripped it. She sat there, waiting for the *warden* to come back so she could possibly have some *yard* time. She imagined she would have to be on her best behavior or she may end up in solitary. She didn't know why that would be a bad thing as she had been alone for so many years. Placing her hand over her heart, she felt it flutter again. She realized why she cringed at the solitary thought, her heart wanted to be with that caveman. Letting out a disgusted sigh, she needed to up her game to keep her distance from him, otherwise she might fall for him and never leave here.

Crossing her arms, she was determined to put up a pretty good fight. If he wanted to keep her here, then she was going to make sure he felt every blow. Then maybe he would let her go out of sheer annoyance. A smile crossed her face as she felt hope in her heart, but soon it was replaced with sadness. Thoughts of him flashed through her mind. Shaking her head, she tried to rid them so she wouldn't back out of her plan of escape.

***

Liam slowly walked to Amara's room. He was still thinking about last night's dream when he finally closed his eyes. Amara asked to see his arm and he gladly rolled up his sleeve to show her. He wasn't sure why she wanted to see it, but she seemed satisfied with it. Before they could continue talking, she slowly disappeared from the dream like all the times prior. He had tried to make her stay, but it never worked.

Licking his lips, her taste on them was gone. He must have licked it all off, as he kept wanting to taste her again. He hoped maybe they could continue their kiss, but he had a feeling she wouldn't allow it.

He was concerned when she looked ill. Hopefully, it wasn't because of him as he didn't want to believe he was vile. He would have believed that if she hadn't relaxed against him and allowed him to continue to kiss her.

Reaching her door, he slowly pulled out the key ring. His hand kept shaking and he had to keep picking up the keys after dropping them. He didn't know why he felt so nervous when it came to her. He figured that they should be comfortable around each other seeing that they had been meeting each other in their dreams since they were kids.

Finally, getting the skeleton key into the lock, he tried to calm his nerves before he went in. He didn't want to start any fights as he was hoping to stay calm and not get her going. As he walked into the room, he could see she was ready to start with him. Letting out a sigh, he knew it was going to be another long day of trying to keep his cool. He raised his eyebrow, crossing his arms as well.

Bring it on, girly girl!

***

"You're such an asshole!" Amara screamed at Liam.

Liam just stared at her face that was red as tomato. All he was trying to do was get to know her and next thing he knew she slapped him. Holding his face, he tried to figured out what he did to deserve such an assault. He didn't touch her or try anything to show he was pushing to mate.

"And you're nothing but a drama queen," he snarled.

She rushed him and before he could stop her, she punched him. Breathing heavy, he tried to contain his anger as his face was still turned. Slowly turning his head, he glared at her. She didn't seem to be fazed by it. As he was about to tell how he really felt, she silenced his vocal cords by slamming her lips on his. Frozen in his spot, his eyes searched for answers, but nothing came out. She shoved him down and didn't let him get a word edgewise.

Liam didn't understand her, one minute they're in a heated argument, the next thing he knew she was kissing him. Now, she laid on top of him as he lay on the grassy, soft ground. Apparently, the argument wasn't the only thing heated as her kissing became more of a need and hunger than the last kiss they shared. The previous kiss was full of need and longing, of the pain and loneliness that haunted him for so long. He worried he passed the onto her, which could explain why she became ill. He didn't mean to. He tried to keep his emotions back, but they ended up flooding into her. He noticed that happened to her a few times in the dreams and he was really good at keeping his emotions back, but apparently last night, he had no control, especially when it came to kissing her.

She cupped his face in her hands, while his hands wandered all over her curves. Her body perfectly fit against his as their make-out session heated up. Occasionally, he would feel her try to pull away, but his hand would rest on the back of her head to keep her from stopping. She seemed to allow him to control her as they continued. As she moved on top of him, he felt his need for her pressing hard against his pants. He so much wanted to go further, but didn't want to push her in case it started another fight. He would take it slow and allow her to steer them that way when she was ready. Maybe his gentleness would increase the chance of her falling in love with him.

***

Amara didn't know what she was doing. She thought she was doing a good job of pissing him off, but something caused her to slam her lips on his. Maybe it was to shut him up, but in the back of her mind, she knew the real reason. In her crazy state, her heart made her want to kiss him again. It felt right before. She even pushed him down on the ground and got on him before he started to fight with her.

She imagined that he thought she was physically fighting with him, but she just wanted to kiss like this. Her body seemed to fit perfectly against his, like a puzzle piece. She wanted to keep kissing him and maybe something more.

Occasionally, her body would try to pull away from him, but his hand always made her stay. Her plan of escape slowly crumbled as they continued. Her hands slowly slid off his face and rested on his chest. She realized she didn't need to hold him in place anymore. He was willing to kiss her back. Before she knew it, his tongue invaded her mouth and chills ran down her spine from this new experience. His mouth muffled her moan and she felt his body tremble. She wondered if he enjoyed that as she hadn't meant to let it out. She didn't want to give him the impression that she wanted something like that.

That last thought finally broke the spell and she pulled away from him. She felt him trying to bring her back, but she resisted him. Shifting down his body, she rested her head on his chest. His breath was shaky, his heart ready to pound out of his chest. Closing her eyes, she tried to calm herself. Of course, it wasn't easy when she felt something pressing hard against her as she moved. It sent her urges into overdrive until she wanted to continued, but she managed to keep her body from moving. He shifted when he laid his head on the ground after holding it up. She imagined he was probably staring at her, trying to figure out why she stopped. His breathing and heart beat started to slow as she knew he was trying to calm down as well. She knew she should get off of him, but she was afraid if she moved then she would start kissing him again.

She laid still even though her body wanted her to move to feel more of him, but she needed to regain control before she lost herself to him. She reminded herself he was the enemy and she was still a prisoner.

***

She's mine!

Liam awoke suddenly, he made sure not to spring up as he felt someone was still asleep on top of him. He shook his head to get rid of the monstrous voice that echoed in his head. Leaning his head back on the ground, he tightened his arms around Amara. He wanted to make sure she was still with him, as in the nightmare it felt like someone tried taking her away from him.

Shivering from the cold sweat that lay on his body, he tried to make sure not to awake her. He quickly wiped his face with his hand to try to hide the evidence of his fear. It didn't work as he forgot she could feel his emotions. He learned this during one of their nightly visits as he believed she was deathly ill. Eventually it made sense when she explained how she was affected by others feelings and had to learn how to build up a barrier to keep herself well. He didn't mean to be that way, but he was greatly excited and felt as if he was on a sugar high when he was explaining the new blade he created. She placed a finger on his lips to silent him and they sat there in silence until his exhilarating feelings went away and they could continue their conversation.

Liam came back as Amara stirred on him and her eyes slowly opened. Before he knew it, she was holding herself up by her hands and he thought he spotted concern in her eyes, but it quickly disappeared when she looked down at her hands on his chest. She got off of him quickly and wrapped her arms around herself.

***

Liam gradually stood up, pretending to wipe dirt off of himself. He tried to avoid eye contact with her as he didn't want to start another fight. Unexpectedly, he felt something soft and gentle. He spotted her hand on his arm before making him look up into her eyes.

"What's wrong?" she asked quietly.

"It's nothing." He patted her hand.

Her eyes narrowed and he could tell she was about to start a fight. Before she did, he decided to smooth it over.

"I'm okay, just had a nightmare," he responded quickly.

That seemed to extinguish the fire before it started. The anger in her eyes slowly disappeared. He was glad she decided not to fight with him. He had no idea why she thought everything was a fight when all he was trying to do was love her, but she seemed content to keep him at arm's length.

As that last thought hit his mind, she did something unexpected. Looking down, he watched her rub her hands against his chest before looking up into his eyes. He saw something in her eyes and thought maybe there was a chance between them. Maybe she was finally getting along with him. The hair stood up on his neck and arms when she pressed her body against his. He was startled by the change of tune from her.

For some reason, their bodies began to sway to invisible music as she laid her head on his shoulder. Her expression showed that she may actually enjoyed being with him. He prepared himself as she gradually moved closer to his mouth kiss him again.

Without warning, he felt extreme pain between his legs. Going down onto his knees, his hands flew down to hold himself. Before falling forward, he let out a groan. Even though he was in excoriating pain, he heard her take off. He would have rolled over to watch where she went, but he couldn't seem to move. It was like her knee was made out of pure steel.

***

Amara didn't know where she was going, but she was hoping to get as far away from Liam so she would be safe. As her feet kept thudding off the woods' ground, she smelled freedom just around the corner. She couldn't believe she did what she did to him. She wasn't planning on it, but it seemed to work to her advantage.

The next step of her plan was to find a way to remove these damn bands. She knew she would have to incapacitate him so he wouldn't be able to control her. At least he trusted her enough to get close and not notice her knee sliding between his legs. He left himself so open that she still couldn't believe it worked. She thought maybe he was baiting her, and then would catch her before she did some damage, but apparently he was surprised by the attack.

Her heart felt heavier as she ran farther away. She tried to ignore it and was almost tempted to head back to him and apologize.

Well almost, she thought.

Her mind flashed memories of them making out, almost causing her to turn around, but she kept going. She needed to get back to her land before it was completely destroyed. She was so focused on running that she didn't hear the next sound.

***

Liam burst out of the brushes and looked around wildly. Sniffing the air, he found Amara's scent again and started to run in the direction she went. He didn't want to run, but he didn't want to lose her either. Of course, his recent injury made it difficult for him to move faster.

As he thought of changing into his dragon form to fly, something caught his attention. Sliding to a stop, he let out a low, rattling growl. Standing before him seemed to be an odd-looking group of men. Sniffing the air, he could tell they hadn't bathed in a long time. Examining them, he would have guess them to be Vikings due to the animal skins they were wearing and their braided hair and beards.

"Ay, and who you be?" the larger man asked.

"Nobody," Liam snarled.

"It seems like you're looking for something, nobody," the man taunted.

"Just taking a leisurely walk."

"Really?"

"Yep."

"Then I guess you weren't looking for a girl?"

Liam lost his cool and almost charged at the men, but stopped when they pulled out their weapons.

"Thought so," the man gloated, whistling he looked over his shoulder. "Hildebrandt, bring thee girl," he ordered.

Liam looked over and saw a scrawny boy pushing Amara in front of the group. Liam growled as she stumbled and fell to her knees. Before he could attack, the young lad picked her up by the hair and drew her against him, his blade pressed against her porcelain skin. Even though she was trying to act tough, her eyes were wide with fear.

Liam wished they weren't in that situation, but in the back of his mind he thought maybe he should let those men do whatever they wanted to her. It'd serve her right after what she did to him. Of course, his heart told him a different story as his mind scrambled to find a way out.

"So, here's what we're going to do. You're going hand over your valuables and we'll keep the girl," the leader said.

"How about a hell no?" Liam growled.

"I wasn't asking," the leader grated.

The leader whistled again, probably the cue for the other men to surround Liam as they began to move toward him. Liam rolled his eyes, not believing those idiots thought he and Amara were simple mortals that they were robbing. Didn't they realize they weren't carrying anything but the clothing on their back? Liam looked over at Amara when a gasp was heard. The scrawny lad they called Hildebrandt dug the blade deeper into Amara's skin.

"I wouldn't do that if I were you," Liam threatened.

"Or what?" the leader challenged.

"This."

In an instant, Liam changed into his dragon form and let out a roar. He thought for sure the men would run away, but they didn't seem fazed that he was a dragon. Letting out a louder roar, he thought that would do the trick, but the leader of the group just let out a bellowing laugh.

"Do ye think we never saw ye kind before?" the leader asked.

Liam eyed him suspiciously. He started to wonder if maybe this group was like hunters, but from a different area. He smiled, licking his sharp teeth slowly. He wanted to make sure they got the message that soon they would be his snack if they didn't go away.

"Ye don't frighten us. We know how to deal with ye kind," the leader taunted.

As the men continued to surround Liam, he growled at them, baring his teeth. If they wanted to have a fight, he'd surely give them one. He snapped his jaw at one man to try to scare them, but it didn't seem to work as all the guy moved out of the way and then continued toward him. Liam decided it was time to go the extreme. He didn't want to, but they were pushing his hand.

Before he could do anything, a chain went around him, dragging him down and slamming his head against the hard, stony ground. As he tried to raise his head, trying to rid the dizziness, a couple of men tackled his neck and slammed his head back on the ground. He attempted to spread his wings, but they were quickly chained against his body. He fell against the ground by the force of the chains pulling it down. Liam tried to struggle out of the hold, but for some reason, he couldn't move. From the corner of his eye, he spotted Celtic symbols on the chains that glowed each time he tried to move. His growls were muffled as they put a muzzle on him. Liam glared at the leader as he placed his foot on top of his snout. He let out another bellowing laugh as a way to gloat in Liam's face.

"By the gods, you will bring us riches," he announced.

Liam tried to jerk out from under his foot, but he was bolted down. He dug his talons into the hard ground as deep as he could go. He wanted to rip the guy apart. The leader leaned in to stare into Liam's eyes.

"Remember this, ye heathen demon, my name is Boris the Terrible and you are nothing against me," he taunted.

Liam tried to growl again, but knew it was pointless. He just made a muffled, pathetic sound. Boris laughed harder. His mind tried to come up with a plan, but before it could, he heard a girly scream. Looking over, Hildebrandt let out another girly scream as he flew up in the air. Liam smiled when Amara let out a monstrous roar in her dragon form.

***

Amara was going to let the men kill Liam, but her heart broke at the thought of losing him. Letting the fire spew close to them, her plan quickly faded. She was going to escape after they were done with Liam, but something in her heart changed her mind.

As a man charged at her, she swatted him away with her tail like an insect. She lifted her front feet up and fell heavy on them to cause the ground to shake, knocking most of the men down. While they were preoccupied, she took a moment to unbolt Liam from the ground. She flapped her wings a few times to lift off and cause some of the men to cover their eyes from flying dust. Before they could do anything, she was already carrying Liam to the clouds for cover. She was about to travel toward her home, but changed her mind when he started to struggle in the chains. She snarled at him to keep still. Eventually, he did.

Amara knew she was going to kick herself for saving him, but she couldn't bear to let him be harmed. A small smile flowed onto her face at the thought of the heroine rescuing the hero. A raspy laugh escaped her.

A quick peek and she saw Liam arching his brow. She knew he was questioning why she was laughing. She ignored him as she continued back to his castle, enjoying the victory.

Chapter Four

"Damn it!" Boris yelled.

He couldn't believe his men lost a dragon. They were going to make a lot of money off its hide. Unfortunately, he didn't realize the girl was a dragon as well or else she would have been chained up first and not watched by his useless son, Hildebrandt. Looking at his injured men, he felt the anger flowing through his veins.

"Come on, ye dogs!" he ordered.

His men groaned as they got up. His eyes landed on his son that didn't stand up. He saw the fear behind his eyes as he knew what was coming next for letting the dragons get away.

Useless boy!

***

Amara hummed happily and Liam knew why. She believed she saved the day, but in fact he allowed her to change as a way out of that mess. He decided to keep his secret as he didn't want to ruin her happiness or start a fight.

If he hadn't allowed her to change, then more likely he would had been killed off and he didn't want to think what those men would had done to her. They didn't seem to notice she was a dragon like him and acted like she was a mortal. A small smile appeared on his face as he was glad she didn't just drop him off at his castle and take off. A quick peek at the band on his right wrist reminded him that he still had some control over her.

The whole time she thought it was her idea to return to the castle, but in fact it was his doing. All he did was send a suggestive thought to her mind and let her believe it was her idea. He had to keep his smile and laugh back so she wouldn't catch on.

As she continued humming, he recalled how her heart had sung to him every night in his dream. That was how they found each other as he followed the tune and soon discovered there was another dragon like him, but a girl. As her heart sang, he felt all the sadness of being alone and believing she was the last one of their kind. He thought the same, but when he found her, he couldn't believe his luck. He thought for sure there weren't any more and they were all extinct.

Liam didn't know how to explain it, but when they got together, there was an instant connection. He felt all of her emotions and sometimes if he wasn't careful, his would flow into her. He tried to avoid doing that to her, especially during the sad times. Her heart song would be a beacon and call to him every night once he closed his eyes, so he never had to worry about losing her.

When he found her in the real world, he couldn't believe she really existed even though he felt it in his heart when they met in their dreams. He couldn't believe they were finally meeting in the real world, of course, her approach was different than in the dreams. In their dreams, they were two beings that knew each other. In the real world, she acted as if she didn't know him at all.

He felt an instant spark between them when they met in the real world, but he doubted she felt the same spark, as she fought with him all the time. He wondered how he could make it work out between them. Maybe a different approach? He tried to recall how he approached her in the dreams after he found her. She seemed excited to meet him and practically talked his ear off which he didn't mind. It was nice to talk to another of his kind who was also around his age.

His parents had long gone, and he never knew where they went when he was a child. They got up one day and left him behind. He grew up alone in the castle, learning what he needed to and waiting patiently to go to sleep to dream of the girl that haunted his dreams for years and disappeared when morning light appeared. He imagined that the girl grew up alone as well, as she didn't speak much about her family. She only mentioned they left her behind to expand their lands and never returned.

Liam retreated from his memories when she almost fell again. He tried to catch her, but she slapped his hands away from her.

"Don't touch me!" she yelled.

He didn't understand the sudden mood swings with her. One minute, she was okay walking with him, the next she acted like he was the enemy.

"I was just going to catch you," he said softly.

"Oh, sure, just like the last time," she said angrily.

"What do you mean?"

"You only caught me so you could steal a kiss."

"I'm sorry, but that was honestly a mistake."

Once those words were out of his mouth, he knew that would fire up another fight. He knew the kiss was something he wanted to, but he wanted it to be when they were both ready. Now, he was wondering if maybe if it was a mistake.

"Oh, great, I'm nothing more than a mistake," she said angrily.

"No, that's not what I meant," Liam said, trying to convince her.

"If I was such a mistake, then why did you bring me here?"

"Would you stop it? Why do you need to stir up a fight all the time?"

He knew he inserted his foot again when her face lost all color and her eyes went wide.

"Oh, so now I'm the one that start fights!"

"Please, don't," he begged, rubbing the bridge of his nose.

"Don't what? Be the one to start a fight?"

"Do this!"

***

Amara was taken aback by the look on his face. She saw something tearing him up inside, but didn't know what. Letting out a sigh, he turned his head away from her to look at something else. She could tell he wanted to say something, but for some reason he wouldn't.

"How about we call it a night?" he said sadly.

Amara was prepared to keep fighting but the look in his eyes stopped her. Before she could stop herself, her feet moved slowly and her hand pulled his face toward her. His body was startled from the sudden impact of her lips on his. Not too long after, his arms wrapped around her, pulling her in tighter against him. She couldn't help but smile. Tingles went throughout her body. She liked how she felt against him.

His mouth took over hers, forcing his tongue between her lips. She accepted without a fight as he pushed her up against the wall. His hand slid down her body until he rested her leg on his hip. A muffled moan escaped her when he began to grind into her. Letting go of her leg, he slid both of her hands above her head before clasping together in his vice-like grip in his hand. His other hand slid down her body again and then up her dress until it was under it and he was holding her leg again.

Amara was the first to pull away which caused him to start nibbling her jawline and down her neck. Her body responded to everything he did as she began to pant, turning her head away from him. She pushed her chest toward him to keep feeling him against her.

"So, am I still a mistake?" she panted.

"No," he answered huskily near her ear.

Amara's eyes involuntarily rolled back into her head when he answered. Chills ran down her spine when his fingers dug into her flesh. He rock harder into her, making her wish there wasn't clothing in the way. Her hands fell when he released them. She kept them on his chest as she was prepared to push him away, but at the same time she wanted him closer to her.

Fisting his shirt caused him to stop suddenly. Before opening her eyes, she felt his sweaty forehead against hers. His breathing was rapid like hers. She didn't get a chance to ask before feeling the sudden coldness between them. Opening her eyes, she saw him a few feet away, just staring at her. Her hand tried to reach out to him, but all she grabbed was air as he was soon gone.

Wrapping her arms around her, she felt even more alone. Her mind was still trying to figure out what happened. Sliding down the wall, she was on the floor with her knees to her arms that were still wrapped around her. As the tears fell, all she could feel inside was complete sadness. She never felt like this before, even for being alone. She tried to cover her face with her knees as she continued to cry.

What is wrong with me?

***

A dragon with red and black scales, flapped its wings a few times before landing. Grabbing a kilt from a nearby stand, two little figures came running toward him.

"Welcome home, Uncle," the girl said.

"Did you find what you were looking for, Uncle?" the boy asked.

"No, I have not, Nikolai," he answered with a growl.

"Don't worry, Uncle, you will," the little girl said happily.

He patted the top of her head. "Thank you for your kind words, Nadia," he said softly.

Nadia stuck her tongue out at her twin brother as their uncle walked past them. The children soon ran after him to keep up.

"So, Uncle, is it true? Is there another female dragon around here?" Nikolai asked.

"I have seen evidence of one, but have no idea where she went," he answered.

"Lord Kane, we found a couple of abandoned children on the side of the mountain," a male dragon said, walking up before bowing with his arm across his chest.

"Children?" Lord Kane asked.

"Yes, the one male child said that their tribe were killed off by hunters," the male dragon answered.

"Let's see if this is true," Lord Kane said quietly.

Walking into the throne room, he spotted two children standing there. The one female with long black hair hid behind the male. Lord Kane didn't like the male too much by the way he looked at him. Something in his eyes told him it would be best to throw them out, but the female made his heart melt. She looked timid and scared. He could tell it had been a while since they ate.

He stood before the boy. "My name is Lord Kane and I'm the ruler of the ice dragons' tribe here," he announced loudly.

The girl hid more behind the boy, but the boy stood his ground like he was challenging Lord Kane. Kane gave him a glare that would scare most dragons, but the boy didn't seem to flinch or anything. Looking over at the girl, he imagined that if he did throw out the boy, she may not stay. Kane let out an irritated sigh before speaking.

"What are your names?" Kane asked sternly.

"Vladimir," the boy answered without hesitation.

Just the way he said his name made Kane's hair stand up on his neck and his skin crawl. Looking past Vladimir, he squatted to be eye level with her.

"Come on, dear, what is your name?" he asked softly.

"Amelia," she answered quietly.

Kane smiled, even though she was too quiet and he almost missed hearing her name, he could tell that she was going to be something special. Feeling the stare from Vladimir, Kane stood up and tried to put the boy in his place by glaring down at him, but it seemed like nothing could break him. As a final attempt to get respect from Vladimir, he stomped forward and snorted. Vladimir didn't flinch or moved a muscle. Amelia cowered behind him. Kane stood up straight again and knew he would have to keep a close eye on the boy.

"You two may stay in our tribe, but you must follow our laws," he said sternly.

The boy continued to stare back at Kane, the little girl peeked around.

"Understand?" Lord Kane asked.

They both shook their heads in agreement. He turned toward the one male dragon behind him.

"Get them settled in and then we'll decide who will mentor them," Lord Kane ordered.

"Yes, my lord," the male dragon replied with a bow and his arm across his chest again.

As Kane left the chambers, he felt a tug on his shirt. Looking down, he could see his niece was fidgeting.

"What's the matter, child?" he asked.

"I don't trust that boy," she answered quietly.

"Me either, Nadia," he said.

***

Nikolai looked back at the boy before eying his sister and uncle. He couldn't put his finger on it, but something was off about that boy. Especially when his gaze landed on him, his body trembled from the other boy's glare. He saw a lot of hatred and anger in his eyes and it was as scary as hell.

***

Amara let out a giggle in the dark as her male companion's beard touched a sensitive spot on her neck. He had been nibbling along her jawline until he found the nape of her neck.

Something changed between them. She wanted to feel him against her and have him touch her everywhere. She wondered if it was because she was afraid if she gave herself to Liam then she would lose her male companion. She didn't know what she was waiting for, as she knew she wanted more from him.

It all began simply, as they were having a conversation like they usually did, and next thing she knew he touched her knee. A surge of heat ran through her as her breathing became heavy when they connected through that simple touch. She wished she could see his face to discover if he wanted to go further. As much as she wanted to, she was only able to see parts that the room allowed her to see.

She pulled him toward her to kiss him as she wondered what it would be like to do so. She just hoped he didn't mind her making the first move. As they kissed, a smile appeared on the corner of her mouth as she realized he wanted to do the same. She did feel like it was all familiar to her even though they never kissed or touched each other before. She pressed harder against his lips until he sneaked his tongue into her mouth. She gladly accepted it as they began to hungrily kiss each other. She was really happy he wanted to go further with her as their tongues did a slow dance.

Amara really liked where it was going and hoping that it would never end as she pulled away to allow him to worship her body with his lips. His hand followed her curves until he pulled her tighter against him. She smiled, inhaling his musk off his bare chest.

"You're so beautiful," he whispered near her ear.

She smiled when she heard him say that to her as heat gathered on her cheeks. She couldn't remember the last time she felt so comfortable next to someone. Then she was hit with the memories of Liam and almost doing the same thing with him. She tried to shake those thoughts away, but they kept creeping back to the front of her mind. She didn't think she should be thinking of Liam when she was with her male companion.

She just wanted him to be close to her so she didn't feel alone anymore. Molding to his body, they fit like puzzle pieces that were meant for each other. Her hand brushed against his beard before resting against his face as he kissed her again. His lips were tender with her until she bit his to make him aware, she didn't want soft and tender. She didn't know what took over her, but she wanted to feel the raw power of how much he wanted her.

They used to sit in that dark room and talk, but something changed. She wanted to feel and taste him. Her heart beat hard against her chest as she felt something for him. She just wished that she could escape Liam and find her true companion. She felt the pull as the sun began to rise. A silver tear slowly slid down her face as she didn't want to go back to that horrible place, but stay here with her true companion… her destined mate.

"Please, don't go," he begged.

"I'm sorry," she whispered.

She hated when it happened as he so much wanted her to stay with him. If she could, she would, but for some reason, the sun wanted her to leave that place and her companion. Tears flowed down her face as she felt him trying to hold onto her, but she knew he wouldn't be able to do so.

"I'm so sorry," she repeated over and over again.

*****

Amara blinked her eyes a few times as the sun shone through the window. She didn't know why she came into that room to sleep when she should have run away. Why did she allowed her captor bring her back there? Why didn't she just escape when she had a chance? Letting out a sigh, she became aware she was still feeling the effects of her dream and the male companion. Things were getting heated up, but then the sun decided to bring her back to reality. She was stuck there with an egotistical male dragon that kidnapped her when she could be out there looking for the male companion that had been haunting her dreams for years. She began to wonder what he may look like as she couldn't really see him in the dark room. It was the usually the same thing where they spent hours talking to each other, but she wanted something more and didn't know where it came from until she realized what happened. It was when she kissed Liam and wanted to feel what it would be like with her male companion. She was glad that they kissed and moved further with their relationship. Closing her eyes, she hoped that last night wasn't her last time with him.

Please let me see him again...

***

Liam continued to nibble along Amara's jawline and felt a surge go through him when her hands touched his bare chest. He didn't know what changed, but one minute they were talking as usual, then he put his hand on her leg. Before he knew it, she slammed her lips on his and was hungrily kissing him. At first, he was surprised by it, as he wasn't expecting it, but he didn't mind. His lips moved from hers as he wanted to taste her skin like he wanted to do before in the real world. He enjoyed her taste. He involuntarily pulled her tight against him. He smiled when he felt her sniffing his scent off of his chest.

"You're so beautiful," he whispered near her ear.

When he returned to her lips, she bit his lips as his chest rumbled. He really liked this as he passionately kissed her. Then he felt it, she began to fade away like she had so many times before. He tried tightening his hold on her by wrapping one arm around her so she wouldn't go. Touching her face with his other hand, he felt the heartache of her leaving him again.

"Please, don't go," he begged.

"I'm sorry," she whispered.

After she said those words, she was gone. Liam just held air. He hated that their moment had ended so abruptly that he felt the need to destroy something. Before he could, he suddenly felt that he was being pulled as well. He sighed as he hoped that maybe they could pick up where they left off, but in the real world.

***

Liam rubbed his eyes to rid the grogginess and let out a sad sigh. He hated when the sun rose. It always meant their time together was over. Looking out the window, he liked Amara in the dreams, but in the real world she acted as if he was toxic for her. Calming his heart rate, he prepared himself for what she was going to do.

Here's to hoping…

***

Liam tried to get Amara's attention, but she kept staring out into the distance. He could tell something was on her mind as she didn't even pick any fights with him. When he realized she wasn't listening to him, he tried to get her to argue with him, but nothing worked. He would prefer an angry Amara to a quiet one.

Looking out into the distance as well, a thought slowly crept into his mind. Smiling, he turned to look at her as she rested her head on her hand on the stone railing. The sun helped make her red hair glimmer as it was on fire. It almost made him forget his idea until he shook his head.

Looking at her again, he still couldn't resist her. He tried so hard not to touch her so maybe she would feel the same for him and not just go through the motions. Before he could stop himself, his hand gently rested on top of hers on the stone railing, she slowly looked over at him which almost stopped his breathing. Her red, ruby eyes had such enchanting powers over him. Having to clear his throat so he could speak, he knew what they could do.

"Did you want to go flying?" he asked gently.

Her eyes became wide before she furrowed her brow. He knew she was trying to figure out what his angle was.

"Okay," she replied slowly.

As she looked down at his hand on top of hers, he followed her gaze. He quickly removed his hand, thinking she was going to start to fight with him before they could go. He didn't see anger in her eyes, but sadness.

"But am I allowed to change?" she questioned, looking at him.

He almost forgot about the bands she wore that kept her from changing unless he allowed it. Arching his brow, he wondered if she had figured out that he allowed her to change when those men attack. Swatting away that idea, he wanted to keep the mood on good terms.

"Of course, how else are you going to fly?" he teased.

Her mouth opened like she was about to say something, but it quickly shut. Bowing her head, she closed her eyes.

"As you wish," she said softly.

Liam didn't like their relationship outside the dream. Either she was fighting with him or being submissive. He wanted the girl from the dreams, where they were equal and she wasn't afraid to say what was on her mind. Without realizing it, he nudged her with his elbow. She looked down at her arm before looking at him, surprised he did such a thing.

"Only if you want to," he said, crossing his arms on the stone railing before leaning forward.

A small smile with pink on her cheeks made him believe that the girl he loved in his dreams may still be inside the one in front of him. Grabbing hold of her hand, he slowly climbed up on the stone railing. He helped her up with him by gently tugging on her hand. The wind blew through her hair causing the fire effect to be more prominent. He wanted to stand there and hold her hand, but he could tell she was itching to go.

Before he could stop himself, he found his finger encasing her chin and tilted it toward him. His lips softly touched hers as he gradually leaned down to do so. Pulling away, he could see she was still weak in the knees and in the haze of such a soft gesture. A genuine smile appeared on his face before he pulled her with him when he leaned to his left to fall off the railing.

She floated above him as he held both of her hands. Her hair whipped around as they continued to fall. Letting go of her hands, she floated higher above him. They grinned at one another. In an instant, she changed into her dragon form and flapped her wings as he continued to fall. He slowly turned around and saw the ground getting closer. He willed his body to change and flew up into the sky.

Once he reached above the trees, he looked around for Amara. He became worried that she had taken off. Before he could try to hunt her down, something whooshed in front of him, causing him to move out of the way. Letting out a raspy laugh, he saw how she enjoyed scaring him like that as she wore a big smile on her face.

Amara winked at him before ascending higher. As he listened to her let out a raspy laugh, he followed her. They swam through the clouds like dolphins in the sea. Occasionally, they would shove each other and let out more raspy laughs, teasing and taunting each other. It felt great to be able to fly around in their dragon forms, feeling the wind hitting his expanded wings and watching the sun set behind the big puffy clouds that flooded the sky. He was so distracted by the view that he almost got hit by something. Looking over, he spotted Amara twirling around in the air. He wondered what she was doing and then she opened her mouth with flames coming out. He was amazed by the sight as she was engulfed in them. As she continued to twirl around, her flames formed into parallelogram.

When she stopped, her face quickly turned away as he caught a red tint on her cheeks. Shaking his head, he realized he was staring and his mouth hung open. He nudged under her chin to get her to look at him. Smiling, he was glad she was okay with him like that.

***

Amara couldn't believe she did her flame trick in front of Liam. She was used to doing it on her own and forgot he was with her. Of course, it didn't help that she felt free before she noticed the bands on her that had grown when she changed. She couldn't believe how well they adapted to her body so she wouldn't have an opportunity to escape them. She actually forgot about them, because she was having fun flying around with Liam. She stared at him for a moment as her heart raced. She began to feel different about him as she saw someone that she could spend the rest of her life with.

Remembering the bands, she looked at him differently, remembering he was her enemy. Her mind raced as she tried to figure a way to get away from him so she could find the male companion from her dreams. As a thought slithered into her mind, a wicked smile appeared on her face as he stared at her with admiration. He didn't seem to notice she had something up her sleeve as she prepared to take him out so she could escape. She was about to attack him but something came crashing out of the sky. She didn't have a chance to react as she plummeted toward the earth. Something had her wings in their talons. All she could do was watch as Liam became further and further away. The only thing she could do was let out a mournful howl.

Amara clenched her jaw when her body finally hit the ground. Lying there, she felt the pain spread out throughout it. She opened her eyes and spotted a brown-scaled dragon, staring down at her. She tried to move to fight, but she quickly coiled up again when another mournful howl came out of her mouth. Her right side hurt the most as she imagined she crashed on it the hardest.

When she heard the brown-scaled dragon snort, she opened her eyes to see him examining her. She would have let out a growl or a roar, but only whimpers escaped. She had never been so injured before. The other dragon tried to get her to lie on her belly, but she just whimpered and turned into dead weight. She imagined what he was trying as he used his talons and dug them into her scales to get her to move so he could mount her. She tried to snap at him, but his sharp teeth were on her throat. Her breathing was eradicated as she didn't know what to do. First Liam, and then she was being held hostage by another beast who tried to have his way with her. She tried to move, but the pain was too much for her to bare.

After many failed attempts, he finally gave up. He just stared her down before examining the situation. Then she saw it in his eyes. He was going to carry her away somewhere and have her flesh. Amara tried to beg him not to, but all she could get out were more whimpers and mournful howls. She kept forgetting that she couldn't speak the human language while in dragon form.

After realizing her begging wasn't working, she tried to crawl away, but he dug his talons into her scales again and drugged her back to him. He tried to position himself better to carry her away, and Amara's mind raced, trying to figure out what else she could do. Like an answer to her prayers, she heard the most wonderful sound. Looking up, she saw Liam come screeching down with his talons out.

The weight of the brown-scaled dragon was off of her as she laid her head down in relief. She knew she must have broken a few ribs. She wheezed with every breath. She tried to move again to hide somewhere, but her body gave up on her. All she could do was watch the fight between Liam and the other male dragon.

***

Liam snapped at the brown-scaled dragon as he moved out of the way. He couldn't believe his luck as he and Amara were starting to get along. Did she have some type of magnet on her that attracted other males? Forced to fight with a dragon veteran, all his battle scars showed that he had survived a lot.

What boiled his blood more was when he saw the creature trying to mount Amara? Something inside him snapped and before he knew it, he was charging head on into this battle. He couldn't believe he was doing that, as he usually was tactical when it came to such things. When he saw that Amara was in trouble and that monster trying to claim her and take her away from him, he knew he had to do something quickly.

As he pulled his head back, he realized he didn't pulled it back far enough. The dragon's talons ripped through the scales over his face. Shaking his head, he tried to stay focused on the fight or else it would be all for nothing. Lowering his head, he tackled the other dragon and tried pushing him farther away from Amara. The creature got the upper hand as he dug his back talons into the ground. Before Liam could do anything there was sharp pain into his shoulder. As the other dragon clenched his jaws, Liam felt its teeth going through scales and muscles.

Picking up his front talons, he began to furiously claw the hell out of the creature. Eventually, he let go of Liam. They growled and stared at each other for a while. Liam felt his legs shaking from the blood he lost. Panting, he knew he needed to do something quickly before the battle armored creature took him out.

While distracted by his thoughts, the dragon snapped his jaw on Liam again and pushed him back. Liam couldn't find his bearings. Letting out a grunt, he felt a stone wall on his backside. He tried shoving the creature off of him, but the dragon just kept tightening his hold on Liam's throat. His vision began to blur as his heart beat loudly in his ears. He realized he was being suffocated. Looking over, he saw Amara struggling to lift her head with concern in her eyes. She dug her talons into the ground and pulled herself toward him. He tried to beg her to go back, but his windpipe couldn't function properly from the vice grip on it.

Liam tried slashing at the beast, but he ignored him. Trying another attempt of pushing, he tried to hurry up of it so Amara didn't have to risk her life for him. As he thought of that, he heard a sickening sound. Looking over at her through teary eyes, he spotted Amara as another mournful howl escaped her mouth. After it died down, she pushed herself to keep moving. Liam's eyes widened when he heard something snapped in the trees. He watched in horror as spears fell toward her and then pinned her to the ground. Liam thought for sure she was dead when she closed her eyes. All he could see was blood, spears and the big, black metal trap on her back ankle. He couldn't believe there were hunters' traps out there.

Letting out a growl, Liam found his strength. The creature was soon on his back as Liam snarled. Encasing the other dragon's throat in his mouth, Liam snapped his jaw and listened as the brown-scaled dragon tried to breath before dying. Liam quickly tossed the beast over the cliff's edge like a rag doll. He listened as it plummeted to the ground below but he didn't really care if he heard it or not.

His running caused the earth to shake until he slid to a stop near Amara. Nudging under her jaw, he let out a whimper, believing she was dead. To his surprise, she slowly opened her eyes before closing them again. He had to hold back his excitement as he knew he needed to get her back to the castle to nurse her wounds. He quickly ripped out all of the spears and pulled the chained out of the ground that pinned the metal trap down. Liam tried to be careful as he carried her, but he had to be quick. He just hoped she would make it as he continued to zoom through the air breaking the sound barrier.

Hold on, Amara!

Chapter Five

Halfway back to the castle, Liam almost lost his grip on Amara when she changed back into her human form. As he tried catching her, he made sure to be careful not to cut her with his sharp talons. Twirling around, he caught her and tightened his hold against his chest as he turned around to continue flying. He was so worried about injuring her that he decided it would be best to let her land against his chest to catch her. He quickened his pace as her body grew colder from loss of blood. He could hear the drips of it hitting the ground below.

He quickly changed when they got back, worried he may be too late to save her. Her hand slightly touched his chest, giving him the hope that she was still alive. Placing her gently on the bed, he didn't care if her blood stained it. She needed care right away. He looked around, not sure what to do until the head of his beast followers came up to him with items to help. His hand shook as it held onto bandages. He wasn't sure what to do. He had never taken care of anyone before. His followers took over as he couldn't seem to move, keeping his eyes on her. He couldn't believe he froze when she really needed him.

What kind of mate am I?

***

Liam watched as she slept peacefully in his bed. He had to listen to her breathing to make sure she was alive as it was so soft and weak. She refused to lie on her back and curled up into a ball on her left side. Apparently, she was trying to hide away as she finally woke up enough after they took care of her wounds. He hated that he had to listen to her muffled cries as her tears hit the pillow.

He didn't understand why she was hiding that she was in so much pain. If he could hear her make some type of noise, then he knew she was alive, but for some reason she was determined to hide away from him. She seemed like she didn't want anyone to see her vulnerable. He was just happy she was okay and might survive this. He exhaled slowly as he hoped she did as he couldn't imagine living alone again. If she was the last female, then how could he move on? Not that he wanted anyone else but her, but that would mean doom for his kind if she perished.

When the medicine finally kicked in, he was glad she was able to rest. He hoped for her to be stable so he could take her down to the healing baths to soothe and mend her injuries. But she soon passed out when she couldn't feel the pain anymore. At least, for the moment, she had a fighting chance and maybe when she woke up, he would be able to take her to the healing waters.

Liam could kick his own ass for putting her in that position. If it wasn't for him she would have focused on protecting herself so the traps wouldn't have gone through her scales. Brushing her hair behind her ear, he continued to watch how peaceful she looked. She didn't seem like the same girl that always wanted to fight with him, but just like girl in his dreams.

Closing his eyes, he began to listen to her heart sing its song again to him. As it flowed around him, it felt like his mind was floating. Swallowing hard, he realized she was his drug and he was getting off on her beautiful melody as he became more addicted to each time he heard it. It gave him the reason to live and to find her. He needed her badly. He only hoped she felt the same for him.

Before he knew it, he brushed a kiss in her hair. He softly planted another on her shoulder and moved down the rest of her arm that wasn't bandaged. His tongue sneaked a taste of her before inhaling her scent off her skin. Letting out a groan, his urges were on fire. He so much wanted to bury himself into her, but forced himself to rub his face gently on her arm. He didn't want to disturb her while she rested. Getting up, he knew he would need to take a cold shower to calm himself before he let his body's needs take over.

***

Liam thought a cold shower would help, but every time he thought of Amara, it reignited the urges to the point where it almost became unbearable. Pressing his hands against the wall, his hips started to rock. Lowering his head and closing his eyes, he tried so hard to think of other things, but eventually his mind went back to Amara. He just couldn't get enough of her. Her scent still lingered in his nose, making her feel like she was there with him. Licking his lips, he recalled how she tasted, her lips and skin. Breathing heavy, he clawed the wall as a way to calm down, but his mind wouldn't let him. His exhale came out shaky when he thought he felt her touching his shoulder as if she was climbing in the shower with him. Inhaling deeply, he thought for sure he smelled her scent in front of him. Licking his lips, he wished she was so he could be kissing and show her how much he loved her.

His hand slowly slid off the wall until his fingers were wrapped around his hardened need. His hips rocked faster as his hand kept up with the pace with stroking. He shuddered when he imagined thrusting into Amara. His groans grew louder as his pace picked up. His body shook when he thought he heard her gasping his name in his ear and feeling the warmth of her breath on it. Resting his forehead on the shower wall, chills ran down his spine as he thought how incredible it would be to be to feel her and bury himself in her. Grunting, he thrust harder and stroked quicker as his mind kept up the thought of pounding Amara.

One last push took him over the edge. Panting with his body shaking, he couldn't believe he did something like that. It felt amazing, especially when he imagined Amara and burying himself in her. Letting out a trembling breath, staring at the wall, he wondered if they would ever get to that point or if she would only continue to push him away.

Quickly washing himself off, his body wanted to go lay down with Amara, but his mind told him it would be better if he slept somewhere else. He knew he couldn't trust himself at that moment. He had a taste of what could be and he wanted more.

After drying himself, he quickly dressed so he could go far away from Amara let her rest. His heart pounded against his chest and his mind continued to race. He began to believe he wouldn't be able to sleep tonight. He felt his stomach drop, knowing he wouldn't be able to see Amara in his dreams and maybe continuing what they did in the last dream.

***

Amara couldn't believe what she was doing. As she walked toward her male companion. As she got closer, she heard water running. Biting her lower lip, she wasn't sure if she wanted to or not. Without thinking about it too much, she smiled and slowly removed her clothes. She listened to him breathing heavy as she got closer. She placed her hand on his shoulder to help herself climb into the shower. He exhaled sharply when she did. She smiled even more as he seemed happy to see her. She stood before him as he kept his hands pressed against the wall on either side of her. His hand slid away from her as his fingers wrapped around his hardened need. Watching him stroke himself for a while, she decided to join him. She reached her hand out and helped him stroke. He seemed to enjoy it as her hand wrapped around his. She leaned close to his ear and gasped his name, but she wasn't sure what she said as it seemed like she wasn't allow to know his name.

His body shook next to hers when he stroked for the last time. She pulled him tighter against her as he calmed down. She wanted more with him, but pleasing him wasn't too bad. She smiled, happy she was able to be with him again. Chills ran across her skin when his beard brushed against a sensitive spot on her neck. She moaned.

***

Liam was right, he couldn't sleep that night. He kept going back to what he was doing in the shower. It felt so real even though he knew it was only his imagination. Looking over, he saw Amara resting peacefully. When she started to whimper in pain, he quickly attended to her and provided more medicine to help ease the pain. The only sound he wasn't expecting was when she gasped his name as he stopped what he was doing. She smiled as she seemed content with whatever she was dreaming about. He shook his head to stay focused on what he was doing so maybe she could heal faster. He never thought she would say his name like that let alone dream about it. Elation spread through him as he was glad she did enjoy his company.

Changing her bandages, he noticed it was taking longer for her to heal. Before he placed new ones, he would take her to the hot baths to help soothe her pain and wash her. He was glad she was still unconscious or else she would fight with him about touching her naked body. Every time he thought that, he would roll his eyes. As much as he would like to worship her body and provide such pleasure, he knew he needed to attend to her injuries before that happened. At least, during these times he could be close to her without getting a slap or a glare from her.

As he looked at her injuries, the anger boiled inside of him. He didn't understand why the hunters hate them so much. They didn't cause any trouble or harm to anybody, but their differences from the mortals obviously instilled fear. Of course, dragons could be vicious, but only when attacked. The only times he had to be a monster was when he had to fight against other dragons or hunters that were trying to kill him. It was only self-defense. If he could fight better in his human form, then he would, but unfortunately, his human flesh couldn't stand flames.

If it was up to him, he would stay in his dragon form, but he was trying to live amongst the mortals. Of course, they noticed something different with his kind, even when they hid behind mortal flesh. He didn't know how they did, but they did and began to hire mercenaries and hunters to come and kill them. Shaking his head, he still didn't understand why the mortals felt the need to kill. Like he said before, they never did anything to them.

A thought slowly slithered into his mind. What if other kinds of dragons did horrible things to the humans and that was why they were being hunted? They didn't want to take the time to sort out the good and the bad as it was easier to take care of all of them at once.

Liam let out a growl. He didn't like the thought of others ruining things for the ones that wanted a peaceful life. Even his family had stopped preying on farmer's animals as they began to have their own at the castle so they wouldn't be the monsters the humans thought they were. He had tried to appear human and did everything right, but somehow, they knew and he would have to fight his way out of trouble. A few times before he tried offering help and technology to help local towns, but none of them would take it. They ended up attacking him and running him out of town. He just wished they could all live peacefully together as they would be stronger together than separated.

Looking back at Amara, he hoped that if she accepted him, then maybe she could help him make peace between the townspeople and dragons. Lowering his head and closing his eyes, he prayed that maybe she would stay with him and be his mate. He had waited such a long time for her and she was finally there, but she didn't seem to feel the same for him. He wished there was some way of showing her that he cared and loved her.

Opening his eyes to have his gaze fall on her again, he felt the heartache at the thought of if she didn't accept him. Would he be able to let her go or would he be a monster and keep her trapped here?

Letting out a sad sigh, he knew only time could tell. He just hoped she would heal or become a little more stable before taking her to the healing waters. It wasn't an easy process as it could be more painful than the injuries she had, but at least she would be healed. Hopefully, she would be grateful that he saved her life…again.

Going back to his thoughts, he tried to come up with ways to show her he wasn't the enemy but a longtime lover. As he rubbed his chin, his mind slowly articulated some ideas that might work. A small smile appeared on his face as he went back through some of the dreams he had with her.

***

Lord Kane sat on his throne, brushing through his beard with his fingers. He was trying to figure out how he was going to find the female so she could help expand his tribe. They were slowly fading, and soon it would only be Nikolai and Nadia with the other two children, Vladimir and Amelia. His mind recalled how Nikolai and Nadia's parents perished. Letting out a growl, he hated how those hunters butchered them in front of their children. The mortals thought the dragons were monsters, but in reality it was the mortals that were, seeing they didn't seem to care about others' lives.

What kind of animal would do that in front of children?

A door slamming opened caught the lord's attention. Looking up, he spotted his faithful second in command, Heathen.

"My Lord, we found traces of the female," Heathen said.

"Where?" Kane bellowed.

"In a forest, we found a lot of her blood, but she wasn't there," Heathen answered.

"How do we know she's still alive?"

"I'm pretty sure she's alive, even though she lost a lot of blood."

Kane brushed through his beard again before looking up. "Get the best tracker and find out where she was taken," he ordered.

"Yes, my Lord," Heathen said, bowing with his arm across his chest.

Playing with the braid in his beard that Nadia braided as it was tradition for the females to do so, it was what his mate would have done, but like Nadia and Nikolai's parents, she was killed by hunters. So, Nadia had taken up the task to help do some of the braiding just like the mortal Vikings had done. He smiled as he recalled how she tried to teach the new girl, Amelia how to do it while practicing on Heathen, but it was a failed attempt. He knew that either Nadia or Nikolai would be the next great leader of this tribe once he passed. He hoped not too soon, as he still had more to teach them. It was important to find the female to help create more followers for Nikolai and Nadia.

As he twirled the braid around his finger, he admired his sister for producing twins. It was a rare occasion when twins were born into a tribe of dragons. Some thought they wouldn't make it, as they appeared weak and pale, but he knew by the strength of his brother-in-law and his sister they would thrive. To those skeptical, they did survive and surpass all the other children in training. That was how he knew his tribe would be cared for and safe in their hands.

A chill ran down his spine as the hair on his neck stood up. The image of that boy, Vladimir, made him worry about the future. There was something about him that made him cringe in such a way. In his gut, he began to believe that something bad would happen to him because of that boy. Tugging at his beard to get rid of that feeling, he began to wonder if that boy even belonged to the same tribe as Amelia. She seemed so sweet and innocent and yet he was emotionless and cold as the ice surrounding the castle. He ordered some of his top guards to keep an eye on the boy and make sure he didn't do any harm to others. At least, if he did then Kane could easily throw him out, but he worried Amelia would go with him.

What's a king to do?

***

As Liam walked down the hallway, everything felt different. He quickened his pace, excited to get somewhere. Opening the door, he spotted what he was eager to get to. Amara looked up at him under her long lashes, fluttering them at him.

"Did you need me, my lord?" she asked softly.

His hair on his arms stood up as chills ran through his body. As she lowered her hand, she rubbed her very swollen belly. He was happy she carried his child. It impressed him greatly that she was acting differently compared to when she first came. She was more willing to be with him and they hadn't fought in a long time. Sighing, he was beyond happy with their lives now.

"Yes, Firefly" he answered, licking his lips.

"I see," she said with a smirk.

She moved onto the bed until she was on her hands and knees. His grin widened as she stayed in that position waiting for him. He loved seeing her in that position. Moving behind her, he slowly entered her and she moaned softly. As he began to thrust into her, he fisted her hips as a way to keep him under control so he wouldn't release too soon. Her hand

moved to touch her swollen stomach as her moans became louder. He laid

his hand atop hers. He enjoyed making love to her and liked that she

didn't care if she was pregnant already.

"Will you only bare my children?"

She giggled. "Of course, my lord, I will only bare your children,"

she answered.

Her answer pleased him as he lost control and released inside her.

Collapsing on her back, he panted, loving every part of his life with her.

I will only bare your children...

Her statement made him jerk his hips a few more times as he lost

control of his body again. He couldn't help smiling as he loved hearing

her promise her body to him and only him.

*** *

After what seemed like a million cold showers later from the last

dream, Liam sat on the windowsill, looking out into the distance. Amara

continued to breathe softly. She was doing better. He was thankful that his urges finally extinguished so he could stay in the same room as her. A chill ran through him when he heard something to make his urges burn again.

"Oh, Liam," Amara moaned.

Screwing his eyes closed, he had to keep his body where it was. Tasting his lips, recalling how they kissed as it didn't help in his quest to not disturb her. Finally calming down, he sighed relief, glad that he could control himself. He wondered what she was dreaming to make her sound so hot. Crossing his arms, he continued to wait for her to wake up so maybe he could take her down to the healing waters.

***

Amara didn't know how she got back in the shower with her male companion again, but she was glad that she allowed him to enter her this time. Apparently, he couldn't wait to kiss her when she showed up and was touching her everywhere with either his hands or his lips. She loved how he worshipped her body as she reached out and pull his need for her toward her. Air quickly escaped her when he slowly pushed into her. She didn't expect such a reaction and she bit down on her lower lip to keep from making a sound. He stilled as she wondered why he did. Her body shook as she listened to his heart beating harder and louder.

"You feel incredible," he said huskily in her ear.

"Please, don't stop," she begged.

She was grateful that he began to move in and out of her as she wanted to feel what it was like to make love with him. She thought about doing this with him since the first time they kissed. She knew they were meant for each other when she felt him searching for her. He pulled her tighter against him as she gasped from the chills running down her spine. She couldn't believe it was really happening as tears slowly flooded her face. He wasn't hurting her, but she knew that being a prisoner at Liam's castle, she would never find her true mate.

As he continued to thrust into her, she couldn't help but moan out his name. That caused him to release inside of her. She didn't hear the name she moaned out, but she didn't care as she relaxed against him. She began to get used to being close to someone that she couldn't imagine being alone ever again. She just wished she could find her male companion as easily as in her dreams, but in reality, she had no idea how she was going to locate him.

Amara trembled at the memory how that other male dragon tried to mount her and take her away to his home. Even though, she didn't like the idea of Liam saving her, at least he was the lesser of two evils.

Before she could enjoy being in the arms of someone she loved, he faded away until she was left in a dark room. Her heart ached for him, but she knew it must be getting close to morning if he was gone. Usually, she was the first to leave as she now knew how he felt when she did.

Closing her eyes, she waited until she woke up. Her chest became tight, wondering why she hadn't woken up yet. Slapping herself, even the sting on her cheek didn't do anything. Pacing around in the dark room, she wondered what she could do to wake up. Thoughts raced through her mind that had a common theme. What if she never woke up? What if she was trapped there forever and could never leave to find her male companion? What was she going to do if she was actually dead and trapped there, never to enjoy the love she felt for him?

Then she felt it. Letting out a sigh of relief, she was glad, because she was just working herself up over nothing. Closing her eyes, she knew she was about to wake up. Even if it meant she was still trapped at least she wouldn't be there in the dark by herself.

***

Opening her eyes, she spotted Liam sitting on the windowsill with one knee bent and his forearm resting on it. He was just staring out the window, not realizing she was awake. Moving a little, she felt her injuries. She noticed they were nicely bandage and she was wearing one of his shirts. Quickly sniffing the collar, she confirmed it was his. She was impressed that she was well taken care of, even after all the hell she had given him.

Trying to sit up, she let out a muffled cry. She thought she could be quiet and maybe sneak out of the room, but he heard her and was by her side in seconds.

"You should rest more, Firefly," he said softly.

She swatted his hand away from her. "I rested enough."

"I was only concerned with your health, Firefly," he insisted.

She glared at him, believing he was making fun of her after doing her flame trick in front of him. She growled at him, showing she wasn't pleased with the nickname. Unlike her dream companion, she knew Liam wasn't being sincere or loving with the pet name. Only her male companion could call her that, not a caveman.

"I'll be fine," she snarled.

She saw a flash of hurt in his eyes, but it disappeared. Letting out another sigh, she knew she didn't need to treat him that way. Even though he kidnapped her, at least he was kind enough to treat her injuries and not take advantage of her like so many other males wanted to.

"I'm sorry," she mumbled.

"It's okay."

His response was almost muffled enough that she would have missed it if she wasn't listening carefully. She knew it wasn't okay. She treated him like the enemy and all he had done was treated her like a lady. Well, except for the times they were fighting. She could tell he was holding back most of his anger, but at least he never raised a hand to her. Another thing that kept getting her going was when he kept calling her a pet name for some reason. She would glare at him, but it never deterred him. She was convinced he was making fun of her because of her fire trick. If she could go back in time, she would have made sure to keep it to herself so he wouldn't be making fun of her.

"Seeing you're awake, maybe we could try the healing waters for the rest of your injuries?" he suggested.

"Sure," she agreed.

Before she could stand up on her own, he picked her up. Going stiff, she wasn't sure what he was doing, but realized he was just carrying her to the healing waters. She figured while he had her, she snuggled against him to keep warm.

***

Liam's body stiffened when he felt her pressed against him. Looking down, she seemed content. He thought for sure she was going to fight out of his arms, but he figured it would be better to carry her to the healing waters instead her hobbling down to them. He was surprised that she didn't say anything else to him to start a fight. Letting a quick, small smile appear on his face, he was glad that she was finally be acting like the girl in his dreams.

***

All Liam could do was hold Amara in the healing waters and watch her struggle and scream in pain. He always hated that part. Even though the waters healed his kind, it was always a painful experience. He didn't understand how something meant for good could be so traumatic.

After her screams died down, she nuzzled against him. His heart pounded in his ears as his urges began to flare up again. Her touch on his bare chest sent tingles throughout his body. Letting out a shaky breath, he leaned down and brushed a kiss through her hair. Her eyes quickly sprung open and the ruby color of them stared into his. He couldn't move, let alone breathe as she seemed to be staring right into him. His knees began to wobble and he was afraid he was going to drop her. As he began to move so he could place her down somewhere, she shifted in his arms.

His eyes widened and his body became stiff again. Eventually, he got used to her as he leaned more into the kiss she had started. Finally, feeling her body, he felt her arms wrapped loosely around his neck. As he was enjoying that simple kiss, she upped the ante and began to kiss him hungrily.

His feet began to move toward the edge of healing waters. Laying her down gently, she spread out onto the soft, moss covered ground. He couldn't remove his eyes from her as the shirt she was wearing clung tightly against her skin, revealing everything. Before he could stop himself, he leaned down and began flicking his tongue causing her nipple to harden. Engulfing it into his mouth, he heard her let out a moan, arching her back. His arms quickly wrapped around her to keep her close so he could continue to suckle her.

Pulling away, he moved so he could do the same to her other nipple. She reacted the same, but her moan was louder. Looking up, he spotted her eyes closed. He could tell she was really enjoying it. He pulled away again when her hands slid up and began to unbutton the shirt she was wearing. She quickly pulled it opened to reveal what he had seen before while washing her. His mouth began to water at the porcelain-colored breasts.

All he could do was stare down at her body she was offering to him. He had dreamt about this moment, but couldn't move. Her hands gradually slid through his hair until they rested on the back of his neck. Pulling him toward her chest, he opened his mouth slowly as he was inches from his destination.

It was as if electricity shot through her body as her back arched again and she let out a scream of pleasure. Chills ran throughout him as he tasted her flesh. He couldn't believe it was really happening. He wanted her so much, his hardened need was about to burst through his pants. He tried to calm it by grinding into her, but it wasn't satisfied with being covered and not being able to be in her.

She tugged at his hair in her fisted hands, causing goose bumps to spread across his skin. Picking her up until she was astride his lap, he moved onto her other nipple. His hands slid down her back and gripped her ass, causing her to squeal and pushed against him more.

He rocked against her as she pulled his mouth away from her nipple and slammed onto his lips. Her tongue invaded his mouth before he could comprehend the change of the situation. He was taken aback from the aggressive kissing until he realized she was showing how much she wanted him. Kissing back harder, he wanted to let her know how much he wanted her. She accepted his lips, which vibrated from her muffled moans.

Liam tried to keep her against him, but she pulled away, tilting her head back to scream out in ecstasy. She collapsed against him, resting her head on his shoulder. Her body quivered against him as he wondered what happened. As she let out a satisfied sigh, he realized that he made her come against him. He didn't realize he was pleasuring her with all the rocking and grinding.

Looking over on his shoulder, she snuggled with her eyes closed. Once she was comfortable, she breathed softly. He had heard both of their hearts pounding away during that moment, but it was only his and she seemed so relaxed and calmed in his arms.

Wrapping his arms tightly around her, he enjoyed feeling her close. She seemed to fit perfectly against him. A small smile appeared on his face. Maybe there was hope for them. Looking up at the caverns, he really hoped there was a chance for them because he never wanted to be alone again.

Chapter Six

"Would it be okay if I kiss you here?"

Amara never thought this male dragon would want to do such things with her.

"Of course," she grinned.

She felt his beard against her skin as he kissed her shoulder. Closing her eyes, she really enjoyed the tender touches he placed.

"How about here?" he asked, his finger on a lower part of her shoulder.

"Yes," she panted.

"And here?"

She moaned in response to his lips on her chest. As he moved his beard tickled a sensitive spot causing her to giggle. He licked up behind her ear before biting her earlobe. She moaned as she tried to offer her body more to him. She hoped they could continue and do more than the last time they were together.

Without warning, the dark room changed into a wooded area. She searched the area and realized her male companion was gone. Boris walked out of the woods grinning maliciously. She couldn't move. She didn't know what was wrong with her, but for some reason she couldn't do anything, not even shift into her dragon form. Her hands covered her mouth as a gasp already escaped her. Boris held up something that made her want to look away but she couldn't. All she could do was stare into two pale emerald eyes. The color was gone from Liam's face as Boris held his head up by the hair to taunt her.

Silver tears poured down her face. She couldn't believe it was true. She may not have liked Liam, but she didn't want him to end up dead. She stilled her breathing when she heard him something that made her blood run cold.

Death to all monsters!

***

Amara jerked awake. She couldn't move much as she was still tightly against something. Looking at her hand, she saw it rested on a bare chest. Her eyes followed the path until she was looking into two emerald green eyes. Before she could fight her way out of his arms, his fingers softly stroke her cheek.

"Are you okay, Firefly?" he asked gently.

All she could do was nod. She couldn't seem to give a verbal response to him as her body and mind were frozen inside his arms. She spotted fear in his eyes as they kept her in place. Before she could stop herself, her mouth opened.

"Are you okay?" she asked.

"Yeah," he answered before gently taking her hand and kissing it.

There was fluttering in her chest as her body was surprised by such tenderness from him. She thought for sure he would be a brute, but the man before her seemed to care so much for her.

***

Liam felt her jerked in his arms and thought for sure she was having a nightmare. He had been awake for a while. He had the same nightmare again about the male dragon claiming Amara as his own. He still shuddered at the phrase that the other male dragon hissed out, echoing in his head. Trying his best to hide his fear from Amara, he decided it would be best to comfort her. She didn't seem to be buying it as she shifted in his arms. He just wanted to keep holding her so she was closed to him, but she seemed to have other plans.

"You can tell me," she insisted.

He let out a sigh. "I know. I just don't want to trouble you with my problems," he said softly, stroking her face with his fingers.

***

"What? You don't think I could handle it? What am I a damsel in distress?" her voice rose.

Before she could continue to fight him, he pulled her in tighter against him. She was going to push away from him, but she felt something that made her freeze in her spot. His breathing became shaky as his heart was pounding against her.

Oh my God, he's trembling!

***

Liam wasn't prepared for his reaction. As she was about to start a fight, he just couldn't deal with it at the moment and did the only thing that came to mind. He knew she could probably feel his body shake and his heart pound, but he didn't care. He was afraid that she would be taken away by the one from his nightmares. It wouldn't be fair, as he had worked so hard to get to know that rare gem only to have someone else come along and rip her away from him.

He didn't want to be alone anymore and hoped maybe she would understand and stay with him. He just wished the nightmare would go away and she would just stop trying to fight with him. Even though, at times, he liked the challenged, there were other times where it was a bit too much, even for him. He just wanted the girl from his dreams.

***

Lord Kane shoved open the heavy wooden doors as if they were nothing but air. He couldn't believe what his second-in-command had told him. As he entered the throne room, he spotted Vladimir surrounded by a group of his strongest men. He thought they were going overboard, but what he just heard, it wouldn't surprise him.

"What have you done?" Lord Kane ordered.

"What needed to be done," Vladimir hissed.

"Why did you feel the need to do such a horrific thing?" Lord Kane questioned with disgust in his voice.

"Those village people were selling that material to the hunters to harm us," Vladimir explained angrily.

"They did nothing of the sort."

"They did so. Humans can't be trusted."

"They could have. They had never done so in the past."

"They would do anything for their precious money."

"They were content with what they had. We would have never done what you had done."

"You would have if you saw your parents, family, and friends all killed right in front of you."

Lord Kane was taken aback by Vladimir's last statement. He now knew the hell the boy had been through. Shaking his head, it still didn't make what Vladimir did as acceptable.

"We work as a tribe, not a single unit," Lord Kane bellowed.

"You're weak and the tribe should have done something about it," Vladimir challenged.

"Killing and destroying the whole town isn't the right thing to do!"

"They all needed to die before they knew that metal could harm us."

"You're wrong. They already knew that metal was harmful to us. That is why they guarded it, to make sure it didn't fall into the wrong hands. They were good mortals."

Lord Kane watched the hatred build in Vladimir's eyes. He could tell the boy would be a challenge. Before he let his anger take over, he stilled when he saw Amelia peering around the back doorway. Looking at her calmed the anger inside of him. He knew if he did anything to the boy, it would harm her. His decision would bite him in the ass later, but it was the only decision he had at the moment.

"Take him to solitary confinement." He looked down at Vladimir. "He has some thinking to do," Lord Kane ordered.

As the guard dragged Vladimir, Lord Kane felt the hair on the back of his neck stand up from the glare he got from him. Swallowing hard, he knew the future he had in this tribe would soon come to the end if he couldn't change Vladimir.

Spotting Amelia trying to hide away, his heart broke even more, knowing she wouldn't be able to survive on her own if he threw out Vladimir and her. He was about to invite her over, but she quickly ran away. Alone in the throne room, Kane scratched his hairy chin, hoping he was doing the right thing. He turned to sit on the throne as he had a lot to think about.

Closing his eyes, he recalled the news he received. Vladimir decided on his own to fly to the one town where the people that were mostly gypsies were keeping the material from the earth from falling into the wrong hands. If made into steel or metal, then it could cause harm to his kind. Lucky for him, the people believed that every life was precious, even dragons.

Now, he felt guilty for showing the town to the new children. He just wanted them to know that they didn't have to fear all mortals, but apparently Vladimir had his mind already made up about them. He knew he had to go see the damage, but at the same time he didn't want to believe such a thing happened. Getting up from the throne, he rushed toward the doorways.

"Let's go! We have damage control to take care of," Lord Kane ordered the others.

***

Liam and Amara flew above the clouds in silence. He suggested that they go for a flight to help clear their minds. They could barely look at each other without feeling each other's fear. He hoped it may help break the ice between them, but it just made it worst.

***

Occasionally, Amara would peek over at Liam. She noticed he was deep in thought. She wanted to say something in his mind, but she couldn't find the right words. Letting out a raspy sigh, she was all mixed up inside. She wanted to go home, but at the same time she wanted to stay with him.

Before she could go further into all of her thoughts of what to do, she smelled something. Her head whipped around wildly, searching. Once figuring where she was, she dived down to the earth below.

***

Liam looked over in time to see Amara descending. He quickly followed, wondering what she was doing. He hoped she wasn't trying to escape again, but in the back of his mind he knew she wasn't. He searched below to make sure she wasn't charging at some hunters, but as they got closer, he saw the destruction of a town. Shock hit him. He didn't understand why the town was destroyed.

Amara quickly disappeared in the dark, gray smoke. He tried to keep up with her, but lost her when he landed. Examining the area, chills ran across his scales as his stomach dropped. He could tell a dragon was responsible for the destruction.

Walking around gingerly, he realized they shouldn't be there. He stepped on something and looked down to see a pile of clothing.

Swallowing hard, he continued to be careful, as if he was walking through a cemetery.

His eyes finally fell on Amara as she stood frozen. Walking until he was standing next to her, she seemed to be staring at something. He followed her gaze and spotted a pair of clothing under a beam. Sniffing the air, he smelled the human's scent. He looked over and saw her silver tears pouring from her eyes before she looked at him. Nudging under her jaw, he wondered what was wrong. Before he could ask, she sent him a message in his mind.

It's Madelyn. She was my friend.

Liam slowly looked at the remains of clothing and knew the human meant a lot to Amara. Her head sprung up as did his. He knew she heard the same sound as he did. They looked at the end of the road where a boy stood. The boy had blood dripping down his forehead and Liam could tell he was seriously injured. Before he could offer some help, the boy's eyes changed from sadness to anger. He let out an angry battle cry before charging at them. Liam got in front of Amara and let out a growl. As the boy got closer, Liam was about to take care of him until Amara got between them. She looked at Liam with those sad eyes and knew he needed to back off.

Looking down, he watched as the boy tried causing harm to Amara's leg by punching it. She wasn't even fazed by it as he continued until his cries slowed down his swings and he crumbled to his knees. Amara let out cooing noises before nudging the boy. He just continued to cry harder before wrapping his arms around her snout.

Liam looked around and couldn't believe that this boy was the only survivor. Watching the interaction between the boy and Amara, he wondered what their connection was. He sniffed the air and sensed that this young child was different than the other mortals, but he couldn't put his finger on it.

***

Liam flapped his wings a few times before landing softly on the ground. He didn't want to wake up the boy wrapped up in Amara's tail. She was trying to keep him warm as it started to become dusk and chilly out. Liam had travelled around to find a doctor that could help the boy. Amara was very concerned about his well-being and seemed shocked that the boy didn't heal from his injuries quickly. Liam asked her why telepathically and she sent him a message in his mind.

This boy has part of my heart in him. His name is Gordon.

When Liam learned how important Gordon was to her, he knew he needed to do something to help out. Unfortunately, they wouldn't be able to keep him with them as others may try to come and kill him. Plus, they wouldn't know how to raise someone like him.

Snorting, Liam let Amara know that he found a place. He carefully gripped Gordon's shirt and placed him on Amara's back. As she tried to move, Gordon slid off and she caught him with her snout. She looked at Liam and knew it was going to be difficult to get him anywhere while on her back.

Leaning onto her back feet, she let Gordon slid down her snout and land into her front legs and pressed him against her chest. After making sure he was secure, Amara flapped her wings and they were off. Liam kept peeking over at Amara with the human child as he wondered what could have cause such a dragon to destroy an innocent child's life.

As the moon peeked from behind the clouds, her red scales glimmered in its light. His mind articulated a different image of her as she carried the child close to her to protect him from any harm from the outside world. A small smile slid onto his face as thoughts about how compassionate she would be if they had children. She was so protective over Gordon, a boy who wasn't exactly like them, that maybe with their own she would be a fierce beast to face if threatening their offspring.

Looking forward, he liked the thoughts about their life and offspring. She would definitely be the one he wanted by his side, not as an enemy. He recalled some of their fights where there were times he almost stepped back from her fighting spirit and fierceness. She terrified him when she glared at him and wasn't backing down from winning a battle with him. He didn't know why he wanted her when she didn't want to be with him, but he knew it in his heart, she was meant to be with him.

Swooping down, she held onto the child tight so he wouldn't fall. They flapped their wings a few times before landing softly on the ground. Liam looked toward the cabin and saw the lights were still on. Looking over at Amara, he saw her eying the area suspiciously, pressing Gordon tighter against her. Liam snorted at her to remind her of why they were there. He tilted his head toward a soft grassy area for her to place the boy. When he looked back at her, he could tell she didn't want to leave him, but after a few raspy snarls and snorts, she finally moved toward the area he gestured at.

He watched her closely. She wanted to back out. She gently placed him down and pulled a blanket from a nearby clothesline with her teeth. Just like she was tucking him into bed to sleep, she tucked the blanket around him to make sure he wouldn't be cold. To his surprise, she quickly changed into her human form to brush some of Gordon's bangs back before placing a soft kiss on his forehead. Before he could stop her from doing anything else, they both turned their heads toward a door opening. She quickly ran away and changed into her dragon form as they both flew into the sky.

***

"Who's there?" an older gentleman called out.

All he could hear were crickets. Before he went back inside, he spotted something wrapped up in a blanket. Moving toward it cautiously, he picked up a log in case he needed to defend himself. Removing part of the blanket, his eyes widened when he realized what it was.

"Martha!" he shouted.

"What is it, George!" she called out, drying her hands on a towel.

"Get my medical stuff ready, we have an injured child!" he exclaimed.

She quickly ran into the house as he picked up the boy. His mind was on doctor mode as he knew he had little time to help this boy.

***

Amara didn't like leaving Gordon behind, but she knew she couldn't keep him with her. He needed to be with his own kind, even though he had a small part of dragon in him. Peeking over at Liam, she was glad he found a doctor quickly. She didn't ask him to, but he went out of his way to help. She made sure to hide her smile. She didn't want him to know that she was pleased with him and might consider staying with him. He had shown her that he was a gentleman and willing to help, unlike those other male dragons that only wanted one thing. She shuddered from such thoughts, but then goose bumps pricked across her scales remembering the events she experienced with him like in the healing waters.

***

Liam let a small smile appear on his face when he felt happiness from Amara. Flashes of memories of those exciting moments together ran through his mind. He had to close his eyes to calm himself down before he overtook Amara. They were at a good moment and he didn't want to ruin it. He just wanted her to be happy.

***

Boris examined his destroyed traps. He thought for sure there would have been a beast there, but it seemed like there were more than three. Looking at the footprints, he noticed signs of a fight between two of the monsters while the other one was snared in his traps. He wondered if that creature survived, seeing there were big pools of dried up blood everywhere. Lucky for him, but unlucky for the beasts. If one was bleeding, then he and his men would be able to track them. A big wicked smile spread across his face. Two beasts were better than one.

***

Once they got back, Liam made sure to excuse himself. He wanted to feel her against him again. There was confusion in her eyes, but her facial expressions seemed express understanding. He needed to get his body under control before he did something he regretted and lost her forever.

He ended up just lying in bed, staring up at the ceiling with his arm behind his head. He would have taken more cold showers, but his feet led him back to his bedroom. He tried so hard to think of other things, but his mind kept going back to Amara and some of the things they had done together. Letting out a groan, he didn't realize his fingers were wrapped around his hardened need and stroking it.

He kept the pace slow, so he could enjoy it longer. As he was getting close, his breathing became erratic. The images of Amara in his head became more seductive and caused goose bumps flow along his skin. He was almost there as he just needed a little more to tip him over the edge of ecstasy.

Liam practically jumped out of his skin when he felt another hand on him. Looking wildly at the person whose hand was on him, he couldn't believe he didn't hear her come in. What surprised him more was her hand wrapped his. Before he could say anything, she removed his fingers gently and wrapped hers around his need. He almost went limped.

"I wanted to thank you for what you did for me," she said softly.

Even though his vocal cords were frozen, he couldn't wrap his head around why she was thanking him. Before he could spit it out, her lips pressed hard against his. Liam became lost in the moment as she hungrily kissed and stroked him slowly. His free hand held onto her face to keep her there with him as he really thought he was dreaming all of this. Chills ran down his spine when she began to grind on his leg and moans vibrated against his lips.

Amara began to quicken her pace, both stroking and grinding. Liam wanted to keep kissing, but she soon pulled away as they moaned and groaned together. The way she touched and stroked him caused him to rock his hips to her pace. Letting out a loud groan when she reached the top and smeared the pre cum with her thumb, his body trembled from her touch. His mind was on overdrive as he couldn't believe she was doing this to him.

Before he could say he loved her, he quickly inhaled and his body jerked toward her. More chills and goose bumps spread across his body when her moan fell into his ear as her body convulse next to him. Listening to her pant next to him, his entire body felt like jelly. Moving his head, so his mouth could be near her ear, he wanted to keep smelling her scent and feeling her close to him.

"Please tell me what I did so I could do it again to experience this," he said, out of breath.

There wasn't an answer, but silence and he felt her body go stiff next to his. Wrapping his arms around her tighter, he wanted to make sure she didn't run or pull away to fight with him. Then her shaky breath hit his ear.

"Sorry, that was unexpected," she whispered.

"Are you ashamed of it?" he asked.

"No. I just wasn't expecting to do such a thing."

"Oh."

She pulled away from him. "Oh, please don't take it the wrong way. I did enjoyed it, it was that I only came in here to say thank you, but when I saw you and what you were doing, I just couldn't help myself," she said.

He rolled on his back with his arm behind his head. "I still don't know why you're thanking me."

Liam's stomach dropped when she looked away. He saw tears, hanging in her lower eyelid. He quickly sprung up and her face toward his.

"Hey, I'm sorry. You don't need to tell me," he said quickly.

"No, it's not that. You were kind enough to help me with Gordon. I'm sorry, but I couldn't just leave him like that." She began to cry.

Pulling her tight against him, he began to rock her. "It's okay. He'll be fine," Liam reassured.

Her cries softened before fading away. Lifting her face, they locked eyes. Liam felt that connection spark between them again. He tried to avoid engulfing her lips with his, but she was made the first move. Liam took the invitation and kissed her back. She pulled away after sucking on his lower lip. His eyes searched hers before lowering to stare at her lips. He much wanted to lean forward and taste them again.

As if she read his mind, she had her lips on his. She hungrily kissed him, holding his face in her hands. His urges were on fire as she aggressively kissed and raked her hands through his hair. Before he knew it, he was on his back and she was on top of him, never removing her lips from his. His body began to function as his hands flowed all over her body. As he breathed erratically, he inhaled her sweet scent. His groan was muffled when she rubbed up against his hardened need with her panties.

He wanted to keep kissing, but she sat up. Her hair was a wild mess as she stared down at him panting and with lust in her eyes. He thought for sure she was stopping before it went any further, but to his surprise she wrapped her fingers around him and moved him toward her entrance.

Liam tilted his head back, closing his eyes as she slowly went down on him inch by excruciating inch. His breathing quickened as his mind raced. He couldn't believe it was happening. He dreamt about it, but never thought it would happen. Exhaling sharply, she finally descended completely onto him. He stilled, peeking to see her sitting there, her eyes closed, but her mouth open. He thought he felt her shaking. Not moving, he didn't know if he was hurting her or what was happening until she began to move on him. Tightly gripping her hips, he swallowed hard to keep himself back. He let her do whatever she wanted as she began to ride him harder and faster.

Liam enjoyed the show in front of him as her porcelain breasts bounce with her. Letting his eyes fall between them, he was covered in moisture and disappeared inside of her. Screwing his eyes closed, he had to contain himself as he felt his balls began to clench from such excitement. It didn't help that her moans were getting louder and louder each time she came down on him. His jaw began to hurt from clenching it so hard. He wanted to release as the pressure kept building, but he didn't know if she wanted his seeds or not. It could all be a mistake like the first few times they made out as at the moment this was a great opportunity between them that he would hate it if she thought it was a mistake and fought with him to where she would never let him near her again.

Startled, he felt her hand on his face. He looked up and saw her eyes were hazed over. He could tell she was on the edge with him. Before he could say anything, she began to speak.

"Come with me," she whispered.

After those words fell into his ears, he gripped her tightly against his body when he sat up and jerked a few times into her. He tried to muffle his grunts, but they came out with his shaky breath each time his hips thrust forward. He thought he was done, but when she let out her whimpers of pleasure, his hips rocked again. Holding her close to him, his body was exhausted, but he didn't dare close his eyes, believing it was all a dream he didn't want to wake up from.

***

Amara felt both of their bodies shaking. She wasn't expecting that, but she couldn't deny her urges anymore. Her body was in tune with his and it was an incredible ending.

Hearing his heart pounding loudly in her ears and how tensed his body was, she knew he was trying to hold back. She had been waiting for him so long it almost felt painful. So, she decided she had to do something before her insides ripped apart.

She didn't realize how much they were holding back until they both released. It was a satisfying ending and both of their bodies grew calm and exhausted. She had never felt anything like that in her entire life. Feeling how much he wanted her from his lips, she knew he passionately loved her. Once he opened up, he seemed like a completely different dragon, just like the one she had been searching for.

As she moved a little to get comfortable, she felt the sweat that had built up between them. Letting out a sigh, she was content with her place at that moment. She gently planted a kiss on his chin, feeling him brush a kiss through her hair. Her body shivered causing him to wrap his arms around her more. She felt warmth from him and she was safe in his arms. She had sensed the other male dragons outside, but where she was, she felt that they couldn't get to her.

Chapter Seven

"My Lord, it appears that the female is with a male," Heathen said.

"I see," Lord Kane replied.

"Should we ditch this thought of fetching her and try for another one?"

"No!" Lord Kane yelled, slamming his fist on the throne's wooden arm. "We will just take her from him."

"But, my Lord, what happens if he has an army?"

"Send scouts to check out his kingdom before we charge into battle," Lord Kane ordered.

"Yes, my Lord," Heathen said, bowing with his arm across his chest.

As Heathen left, Lord Kane combed his beard with his fingers. He had another matter on his mind. Vladimir had been causing some trouble amongst his tribe. During solitary confinement, he attacked a guard and badly injured him. Lord Kane wanted to toss the boy out, but he knew that would be unwise with Amelia's life being at stake. How could they survive during the great blizzard that would be coming soon?

Closing his eyes, his skull felt like it was ready to split in half. He had never faced such a tough decision before. He just hoped that maybe Vladimir would get whatever was in his system out so that he could focus more on his new mate.

Here's to hoping…

***

Liam almost had to pinch himself to make sure he wasn't dreaming. He woke up with Amara still in his arms, but she was staring at him. She didn't have the look about her of starting a fight, but the look of a predator. At first, he was a little frightened, but realized it was more for lust than killing.

Before he knew it, she was on all fours, wiggling her butt toward him. It was almost like his dream, but she wasn't pregnant. Without thinking too much into it, he was behind her, thrusting away. Placing her hand on his that was gripping her hip, he glanced down to see her looking over her shoulder at him.

"Harder, Liam," she ordered.

He did as she asked, closing his eyes and clenching his jaw to keep from disturbing the moment before he felt a squeeze on his hand.

"Look at me," she commanded.

His eyes locked with hers, still clenching his jaw.

"I want to hear how much you're enjoying this."

Obeying her again, his jaw opened to let out the groans and grunts trapped behind the barricade. He could tell he pleased her as a big smile spread across her face. Her moans mixed with his groans as he kept rocking into her. Closing her eyes, she turned her head as her wild red mane shook each time he thrust into her. Reaching down, he fisted it and tamed it into his hand. He pulled on it until she was pressed against his front. Her arm outstretched until her hand rested on the back of his neck and her other one slithered down her body until she was rubbing herself below. His other hand fisted her breast as he continued to pound into her.

Liam licked up her neck, tasting her sweetness, causing his urges to flare up again. Goose bumps spread across his skin as her moans got louder. Her body rocked with his making it harder for him to keep his release back.

His body jerked forward more than he intended, forcing her the hand she rubbed herself with underneath her to squeeze his balls. She continued to fondle them, making it harder to hold back. As they moved in unison, his mouth was close to her ear so she could hear his animalistic grunts. This seemed to make her more excited as she puffed out her chest and he pinched her nipple.

As her moan hit a high pitch, he pushed hard one more time before they both released. She continued to scream in ecstasy as he muffled his yell by biting her shoulder. Letting go of her shoulder, he rested his head against her. His legs were shaky and weak as he panted. As she leaned her head back, he felt the sweat on their bodies.

Her body vibrated against his as a smile spread across his face. He loved hearing her laugh, even though it sounded like she was exhausted. She didn't even bother to pull away or make him stop holding her like he was, her hair still clenched in his grip, his other hand on her stomach. As she pushed back against him to clear up the small amount of space between them, her butt cheeks brushed up against him, sending a bolt through his body. He felt the sudden energy to do her again, but he wasn't sure if she was ready.

She slowly turned around in his arm and he released his hold on her. Wrapping her arms around his neck loosely, she planted her lips on his and began gently kissing until it became more of a need. As her hand brushed through his hair, his fingers danced across her curves. It was a clear sign that she wanted to go again.

A grin tugged at the corner of his mouth. He was ready and willing do to as she pleased.

***

Liam had Amara pressed up against the stone wall, making out. He was giving her a tour of the castle when he realized that he didn't need to keep the bands on her anymore. Once those silver bands hit the ground with a loud clinging sound, she was in his arms in seconds.

He slid his hand up her dress as her leg continued to rest on his hip. He loved feeling her flesh and was glad she decided to stay with him voluntarily. Pulling away from her, so his thumb could gently rub her swollen bottom lip, he stared into her eyes.

"Stay with me," he whispered with a little begging behind his voice.

"Yes," she answered quietly.

As he leaned in to kiss her more, he watched as the smile disappeared and distance grew in her eyes. He felt his stomach drop as his mind raced to figure out what was going on.

"What's wrong?" he asked quietly.

She let out a sigh. "I'm sorry, I'm just worry about my homeland," she answered, lowering her eyes.

He lifted up her chin. "I set you free," he said softly.

"What?" she asked, searching his eyes.

"You are free, Amara," he answered.

***

Amara thought she heard him correctly the first time, but she heard the sadness in his voice. Looking into his eyes, she could see the fear behind them. She knew he was worried she wouldn't return. Even though, he had kidnapped and held her prisoner, she couldn't stay away from him too long. She just wanted to make sure that her family's land was safe and sound.

Biting her lower lip, she felt so torn inside. She was afraid of going to her homeland in case her mind decided to stay and not return to Liam. There was also the possibility that it was overrun by mortals and hunters where they would capture her and Liam would never know of what really happened to her. More likely, he would have thought she ran away from him.

A tear slowly slid down her cheek. She didn't mean to start crying, but she felt the overwhelming sadness that he would experience if she disappeared out of his life. His eyes left hers as he watched the tear fall from her cheek. Exhaling sharply, closing her eyes, he slowly wiped the remnants of the tear from her cheek with his thumb. She had to grip onto his arms to steady herself as her body shook. Her legs didn't have the strength to hold her up anymore.

Leaning forward with her head down, she tried to calm herself, but she couldn't seem to get enough air and began to hyperventilate. At least, he was steadying her so she wouldn't crumble to the floor. She had no idea what was going on. Her emotions overwhelmed her. She had never felt that way before. Her eyes widened as she slowly looked up into his face. Even though his face was a stonewall, his eyes gave him away. She started to realize she was feeling his emotions, flooding and mixing with her own.

Looking back at the ground, she inhaled and then exhaled slowly to try to calm her body and hopefully get everything under control again. She recalled being overwhelmed before and feeling ill. Now, she knew why. He had the ability through some type of connection to push his emotions into her and vice versa. She didn't know how he could remain stoic as he should be reacting the same.

Startled, he pulled her tight against him. She felt her breathing and heart become calm. Snuggling into him, she felt relaxed and calmed in his arms. He shifted his weight against her and felt his hot breath against her ear.

"I'm sorry. I need to learn to control myself," he whispered.

"It's okay," she said softly, closing her eyes.

His blood hummed a sweet lullaby in her ears as his heart calmly pounded against her chest. She could easily fall asleep to the tune, but a thought hit her like lightning bolt. Pulling away from him, she saw the concern in his eyes.

"I should go and check on my homeland," she murmured.

"Sure," he said softly, sadness in his voice.

She slowly pulled more away from him until their fingers barely touched. Amara eyes locked on his. She felt like that would be the last time she would see him. Quickly turning around, she tugged her fingers out of his. As the tears continued to fall, she held up her dress so she wouldn't trip on it. She didn't need to be clumsy at that moment for him to save her again. She had to rush to make the distance between them or else she would never leave. Determination filled her heart as she knew she needed to see if those mortals had done anything horrible to her family's land.

***

Liam watched as Amara faded into the distance. He couldn't believe how quickly she wanted to get away from him. Looking down at the bands, he wondered if he made a mistake or was fooled to believe she wanted to stay with him. His heart sank deeper into his chest. He had to hold back his feelings or else he would make her ill again. Letting out a sad sigh, he just hoped he made the right decision.

***

Boris watched as the forest burned. A wicked smile spread across his face. He figured that would bring the beasts to him. He had his men scare and kill some of the animals living here. They had a big celebration that polluted the streams and plant life. They cut down the trees to make bonfires all around them so those creatures wouldn't get a jump on them. If that didn't draw out those beasts, then he may have to go down another road. Looking over at his son, Hildebrandt, the boy's brow furrowed. A bellowing laugh escaped him as he figured he would be somewhat useful as bait, even if he was scrawny. It would be some type of meaty treat for those monsters.

***

Amara kept flapping her wings as if she was trying to get away from Liam, but it didn't seem fast enough. The tears continued as she tried to hold them back, but the dam was broken open and they continued to pour down her face. Closing her eyes, she knew she needed to check on the land and then she could return to Liam.

Something hit her nose that made her eyes widen. Looking down, she was horrified by the scene below. Her precious land was ablaze. Her mind scrambled, trying to figure out what to do. She kept flying around to see if there were any survivors. All she saw were carcasses and scorched trees. The sadness quickly faded, replaced by anger. She flew closer to the rising flames as her scales prevented it from burning her. Clenching her jaw, she wildly looked around to see who was responsible for all of this.

Through the flames, she spotted a familiar figure. Flapping her wings gradually, she descended slowly until her feet touched the ground. She let out a low, rattling growl at the figure. She would like to slice the smirk from his face.

Boris didn't seem fazed by her dragon form. "About time ye showed up."

Amara could easily take one bite and he wouldn't exist anymore, but sounds around her caught her attention. She spotted his fellow hunters surrounding her. Letting out another low, rattling growl, she enjoyed scaring the scrawny lad next to Boris. Boris shot him a dirty look as Hildebrandt lowered his head, ashamed. Amara could see there wasn't a very good relationship between these two, but she saw some resemblance between them.

Before she could attack, a chain netting fell on her. She struggled to get out of it, but the men quickly subdued her and bolted the net to the ground. She snorted at Boris as he stepped closer to her. Digging her talons into the ground, she tried to push herself closer to him so maybe she could do some type of damage. Placing his foot on her snout, she let out a small growl.

"Where's the other monster?" Boris asked.

Amara's heart dropped as she recalled Liam. Tears pooled in her eyes as Boris furrowed his brow.

"What's the meaning of this?" he said quietly to himself.

Amara tried to scrunch back to hide her tears, but she was pressed against the ground tightly. All she could do was scowl at Boris, but the silver tears fell, making her appear less than intimidating. Boris rubbed his scruffy chin.

"Interesting," he mumbled.

Removing his foot from her snout, he quickly turned around, twirling his index finger in the air.

"Let's load her up," he ordered.

Amara let out roars and growls as she struggled against the chains. That didn't deter the men from prepping her for the trip. As the tears streamed down her face, she began to let out mournful howls. She didn't know why she was doing that, but she thought maybe Liam would hear and come to her rescue. She hated to ask for help, but what else could she do.

Looking up, she heard an echoing roar in the sky. She thought it was Liam, but as the creature got closer, she realized it wasn't him. Tilting her head to the side, she was confused. Sniffing the air, the beast's scent was foreign to her.

A few more appeared in the sky as the men scrambled around her to get their weapons ready. As one man tried to swing his ax at one of the dragons, the other dragon swooped down and threw the man far away. All

Amara could do was lie there and watch as these dragons took care of the men. She whimpered, unsure what to expect.

One flapped its wings a few times before landing. She stared, waiting to see what they expected. It lowered its head and its powerful jaws gripped the chain netting and ripped it off of her. Stretching, it felt good to be out of that trap. She was about to thank the dragons, but something on the one in front of her changed her mind and she panicked. She knew she needed to get away.

Before she could, she felt one land on top of her and pushed her to the ground again. She tried to fight it off, but something freezing cold hit her scales. She watched in horror as big chunks of ice began forming on her. The one dragon that held her down got up as the ice spread across her. Her body began to shiver from the sudden cold.

Opening her mouth, she tried to shoot fire out to melt the ice, but the dragon in front of her, quickly pushed her snout down with its talons until her chin was pressed against the hard ground. With what little strength she had, she struggled, but they all let out raspy laughs. She knew she was doomed. Even though she was muffled, she tried to let out more mournful howls through her clenched jaw. Tears flooded her eyes, where everything was blurry.

Her heart skipped a beat when she thought she heard something. Sniffing the air, she looked up into the sky. Her heart jumped for joy when she saw Liam descending with his talons out. Her body relaxed.

As he attacked the one holding her snout down, she saw the others surrounding him. Even the ones blowing ice on her had stopped to attack him. She tried to free herself in order to help him, but it was no use. She was mostly frozen to the ground. As a sigh escaped, she realized she could see her breath. Her heart began to beat slowly as her body shivered more. Soon, she couldn't feel the parts of her body that were covered in ice. She tried to make a sound to alert Liam, but her eyes began to feel heavy. As she struggled to keep them open, she watched as Liam continued to fight with the other dragons. Soon, everything went black.

Chapter Eight

Boris put the cold, steel mug up against his forehead. His head was ready to split in two from the headache that attack left him with. Looking around, he spotted his men and heard them let out moans and groans from their injuries. He couldn't believe they were jumped by ice monsters. Usually, they didn't travel so far out, but for some reason they did.

Closing his eyes, he wondered if that female creature was worth more than he thought. Those ice monsters seemed to fight with everything they had to protect her. He knew she wasn't one of them, but she seemed to be something special.

Opening his eyes when he heard metal clanking off the wooden table, he looked over to see Hildebrandt sitting down. The smirk returned to his face as he knew what he would need to do to capture such a rarity.

***

Amara cried out in pain as Liam tried to keep her in the hot bath. He knew it was painful as the cold seeped into her muscles and veins. They were in the larger of the hot baths to help melt the ice away, but it didn't seem to help her insides.

He decided to take her out of the hot baths as she continued to scream like someone was skinning her alive. He had tried everything to warm her up, especially wrapping his body around her, but that didn't seem to work.

She whimpered and squirmed in his arms as he tried to figure a way to help her. Laying her gently on the bed, he quickly ran around collecting every blanket he had. When he got back to her, she rolled back and forth as her whimpers turned into cries. She covered her face with one hand as her silver tears flowed down her face. He quickly wrapped her in blankets and tightened his hold on her. Her cries slowly faded as her teeth began to chatter. As he tightened his hold on her, he still felt her shivering under the ten layers of blanket. Looking at her, he could see the fear in her eyes. Stroking her cheek, her skin was still ice cold.

"I'm so cold," Amara stuttered.

"I know, firefly" Liam said sadly.

"I don't want to die," she cried, still shaking.

"I won't let that happened," Liam promised.

A small smile appeared on her face. He was glad she believed him, because he wasn't sure what to do. His blood boiled thinking of those ice dragons. He didn't know why they were out that far when they stayed amongst the mountains. Lucky for Amara, he was able to fight them off and bring her back to the safety of his castle.

He'd fallen asleep after moping around about her leaving when the same monstrous voice from before woke him with claims that Amara was his. When Liam sprung up from that echoing nightmare, he heard her muffled mournful howl in the distance. Without thinking, he jumped into action.

All he could think about was trying to keep her alive. His stomach dropped when she closed her eyes. He pressed his ear to her chest and let out a sigh of relief, glad she was still alive. Leaving her side for a second, he quickly spit out a fireball to get the fireplace roaring. He returned to her and rubbed her covered arms to help warm her up. His body began to shake at all the thoughts rushing through his mind. He tried to keep his emotions under controlled, but he was worried he may lose her.

Fire dragons never dwell well in the cold...

***

"Hurry up!" Boris yelled the command.

The men groaned as they moved around heavy objects, covered in tarps. Boris looked around and knew he'd chosen the perfect place to trap those beasts. His eyes landed on a big pole in the middle of the opening of the woods. A wicked smile spread across his face. He couldn't wait to hunt the monsters.

***

Lord Kane grew discouraged as some of his men bandaged up their injuries. They were so close to capturing the female, but at the last minute they had their asses kicked by a single male, fire dragon. He wondered why the female was out alone and how she'd gotten captured by some lowly hunters.

As he raked through his beard, he came up with another plan to get the female. It would be risky, but it was the only chance they had for survival. He would have to wait until his men healed before they attacked. One of the ice dragons tracked down the female. Lord Kane was glad that they hadn't lost her forever.

We still have a chance for survival…

***

Amara slowly awoke. Her mind was still groggy and the sunlight hurt her eyes. Blinking a few times, she realized it was morning. Letting out a sigh, she was glad she made it through the night. As the rest of her body woke up, she felt the coldness had left it. Gradually turning to her other side, she noticed she was alone in bed. Sitting up quickly, she looked around wildly for Liam.

Her eyes landed on the fireplace and saw it still roaring with flames. Placing her hand on her chest, her heart fluttered a few times as she thought of the many times he had cared for her. She realized and confirmed something that had been bugging her for a while. She tried to ignore the thought but it kept hinting something she should have known a long time ago.

After descending down the stairs, she gradually checked each room. She spotted Liam as he sat, sharpening a sword, whistling a tune. Leaning against the doorway, she continued to watch him in silence as she didn't want to interrupt him.

Liam pulled the stone away from the blade and blew on the cold steel. Testing the sharpness of it, he slid his thumb along it. He rubbed his thumb and index finger together as he figured he should sharpen it a bit more, just in case he needed it. In the back of his mind, he hoped he didn't, but it seemed like everyone was after Amara so he might not have a choice.

He was about to go back to whistling as his sharpening slowed down. Looking toward the doorway, he saw Amara was standing there. He practically dropped everything to be standing in front of her. His eyes examined her from head to toe when she stood up straight. Before he could stop himself, he had her wrapped up in his arms, thanking the gods she was okay.

As he continued to hug her, he realized things must be awkward as she went stiff in his arms. Pulling away, he saw she wasn't sure about something, and as it shown in her eyes. He lowered his head.

"Sorry," he mumbled.

He felt her lift his chin so his eyes locked with hers. He would never grow tired of looking into those ruby red eyes. They seemed to be sparkling more with happiness than anger. His eyes slowly fell to her lips and saw her chewing on it. His mind halted to the idea of kissing her as his stomach dropped from the possibility of bad news.

She's leaving me!

"What's wrong?" he asked nervously.

He didn't want to ask; he didn't want the answer, but he couldn't stop the words from falling out of his mouth. His fears were confirmed when she looked away from him. At that moment, he felt the whole world was crumbling away. He couldn't believe that he saved her only to have her leave him. Of course, he did tell her she was free after releasing her from those shackles. Picking up her hands, he stared down at them, wishing he had more time to convince her to stay with him. Letting out a sad sigh, he knew what he had to do.

"I understand. You may leave, Firefly" he said softly, sadness in his voice.

"What?" she asked.

He looked up and saw pure shock on her face. She shook her head.

"No, that's not why I'm here," she said.

His mind scrambled, trying to find an answer as he was even more confused.

She stepped closer to him. "I wanted to thank you for saving my life," she said seductively.

Liam's jaw was on the floor. He thought for sure she was leaving him, but she seemed to want to stay with him. He continued to watch her as she got closer and her fingers played with the collar of his shirt.

"But I was wondering if we could have some fun," she said softly before sucking on her bottom lip.

Liam wasn't sure if he heard her correctly as his heart was pounding loudly in his ears.

"Wait, what?" he choked out.

She giggled, and he began to relax. She walked around him until she was at a table. Her fingers slid across the metal bands that she used to wear. Picking one up, she turned slowly to look at him.

"I would like to have some fun," she repeated.

Letting out a chuckle, he walked over to her nonchalantly. She handed him the band as he looked at it in his hand. Looking back into her eyes to make sure he understood correctly.

"So, you want to play, Firefly?" he asked huskily.

***

Amara had to close her eyes for a second to contain herself as the chills ran down her spine. Her urges were an inferno, hearing him talk like that. Locking gazes with him, she didn't want to wear those shackles again, but something deep inside of her found a thrill in his dominance.

His arm slithered around her and pulled her tightly against him. Her hands rested on his chest as he stared into her eyes. Her body shook, not because of fear, but the excitement rushing through her veins.

He leaned his forehead against hers. "Come on, let's go play with fire, Firefly," he said huskily.

She exhaled quickly when he picked her up and toss her over his shoulder with ease. Swallowing hard, she listened to him pick up all the bands before leaving the room. Her mind raced, wondering what she got herself into.

He wasn't wasting any time as he took the steps two at a time. She imagined he would just skip all of them, but maybe he was seeing if she would back out. In the back of her mind, she wanted to get out, but her urges wanted to keep going.

He softly placed her down on her feet and threw the bands on the bed behind her. She never realized how tall he was until he stood up straight. He must have been slouching so he wouldn't intimidate her. Swallowing hard, she liked his overbearing presence. Her legs shook so fiercely she feared they wouldn't hold her up anymore, but she stood her ground so she wouldn't seem weak.

It was becoming hard for her to keep looking into his eyes as they became dark and intense. She was about to look away when he took a step toward her. Her mind told her to get away, but she stood her ground.

"I want you to challenge me," he ordered huskily.

Shivers shot throughout her body from his tone. "What do you mean?" she choked out.

"I like it when you fight me, Firefly," he said sternly.

A wicked smiled crossed her face. Before he knew what hit him, she slapped him. Giggling, she enjoyed his reaction. It wasn't hatred, but like she opened the cage of the predator ready to pounce on its prey.

"So, like that?" she teased.

A smirk appeared on his face before he held up the first wrist shackle.

"Let's play, Firefly," he gloated.

"Yes," she whispered, holding both of her hands up, wrists together.

After clasping one band on, he looked her straight in eyes. "Are you sure you want this?" he asked her.

"Yes," she begged, her breath shaking.

Liam clasped another band on her other wrist before crouching down to her ankles after grabbing the other bands. Amara closed her eyes to keep herself calm. She wanted to get started, but he took his time. She listened to the clasping and felt the cold metal against her skin. Goose bumps ran across her flesh as his fingers flowed soft as feathers. They kept rising ever so slowly and she almost fell forward from leaning into his touch. She moved to kiss him, but he held her in place. Furrowing her brows, she wondered why he didn't want to kiss her.

"Remember, give me a challenge, Firefly," he ordered.

A smile spread across her face as she forgot what they were doing. She shoved him away and he stared at her with that predatory gaze, putting on the band that controlled hers. Without warning, her arms went above her head with her wrists together. He lifted up his hand and she felt herself rise as her toes scraped the floor.

Her breathing shaky, only inhaling sharply, he took each step toward her slowly. As he was inches from her, she playfully struggled against the hold that the bands had on her. Enjoying the show, he let a smile slowly appear on his face. She knew she was doing well at what he asked. In one swift move, he ripped open the front of her dress. She couldn't help but let out a whimper.

Before she could make another noise, he slammed his lips on hers. A jolt shot through her as all her nerve-endings became on high alert.

Pulling away, he rested his forehead against hers, breathing hard. She looked at him and realized his eyes were closed. It was like he was having an internal battle with himself. She didn't want him to be that way; she wanted his raw self.

She struggled against the bands again to get him back to where she needed him to be, both physically and mentally. He seemed to respond to this as a smirk crossed his face. She squealed when he pinched, then twisted her nipples at the same time. Leaning in, his mouth close to her ear.

"You like that?" he asked in a husky voice.

Her body began to shake. "Yes," she panted.

"How about this?" He nipped the nape of her neck.

Amara let out a shaky breath. Arching her back, she was ready to offer her body to him.

"Uh-uh, Firefly, not yet. I'm still having my fun," he whispered.

Amara had to bite her lower lip to contain herself. She wanted him inside of her, but he seemed to be taking his time. Her ears filled with the sound of her dress being ripped off her body. Hitting the ground lightly, she would have missed it if it wasn't for her super hearing, especially with her heart pounding in her ears. Her body shuddered at the sound of his low groan near.

"Mmmm, lace," he groaned.

She gasped when his fingers slid over the lace panties. The rumble from his chest happened before she heard his chuckle.

"Mmmm, you're wet, Firefly," he said in a low tone.

"What are you going to do about it, my lord?" she asked innocently.

He must have liked that as she caught him inhaling quickly before letting out a shaky exhale. His eyes darkening with lust, licking his lips. She tried to calm her breathing, but it was still shaking with thrill when she saw the predator in front of her.

Bending over, he picked up her torn dress. He ripped a strip of the material and slowly walked behind her. Amara had no idea what he was doing until the strip covered her eyes. All her nerve endings reacted to the silky materials on her face. It was so exhilarating that she swore she would come instantly, but she calmed herself a little by thinking of other things, like trees and grass. Another gasp escaped her when she felt his touch on her face. She liked that her sense of touch was heightened when he blindfolded her.

"Easy, Firefly. I want you to feel me before it ends," he ordered in a low tone.

The feathery touch of his fingers slid down her body until it reached her wetness. As she let out a whimper, her body jerked toward his touch. He kept teasing her by pulling his fingers away, making her want him more.

"Please," she begged, her jaw clenched.

"Please, what?" he taunted.

"Please, my lord, I want to feel more."

"Do you?" he teased as he slid his finger inside her underwear.

She let out a slow, shaky moan as his finger rubbed the right place. This caused her to try to spread open her legs more so he could slide his finger right in. But he kept avoiding such an invitation. She began to squirm, but stopped when he didn't rub her anymore.

"Uh-uh, Firefly, behave or I won't let you release," he ordered softly.

Even his breath tickled her skin, making her want to tip over the edge. As he began the process over, she tried her best to stay still.

"Good girl," he whispered.

Her breathing was erratic, but she did her best not to squirm. Soon, his finger found her opening and slowly entered. She let out a shaky gasp as another finger followed. She let out a quiet moan.

"I want to hear you, Firefly," he ordered.

Her moans and whimpers became louder as she moved with his fingers.

"That's right…ride them," he commanded.

Amara could feel she was almost over the edge, but he started to slow down his pace. She squirmed to try to get her back where she was, but he seemed to keep taunting her.

"Please, my lord," she mustered out.

"Please, what?" he asked.

"Please, let me."

"You want to come? On my fingers?"

"Yes, please."

"Okay, Firefly, I will allow you."

After he said that, she felt him deepening his fingers into her. Moans of appreciation passed her lips. As she began to sway with the motion, he placed his hand on her back to keep her where he needed her to be. He quickened his pace and his fingers kept pushing up inside of her.

"Is this what you want?" he asked quietly.

"Yes," she gasped.

"Did you want me to stop?"

"No, please, don't stop."

"Are you almost there?"

"Yes, just a little more, my lord."

"Do you want to come?"

"Yes, please."

"I want you to release on my fingers."

"Yes, oh, God, please."

As his fingers thrust one last time inside of her, her body jerked until it slowed to a quiver. Her moans faded to a quiet whimper as she felt her release shattered her insides. Her heart pounded in her chest as she tried to catch her breath. As another wave of ecstasy flow throughout her body, she released soft moan after soft moan, her body quivering as he pushed into her again.

Her feet slowly touched the ground as her arms went behind her back. She had no idea how he was going to top that one, but he slowly forced her to her knees. Her arm jerked when she thought she was going to lose balance, but her wrists were bonded together. She could still feel him in front of her as his musky scent filled her flaring nostrils. She heard him sucking on something.

"Mmm, you taste incredible," he teased.

Before she could say something there was a scent under her nose.

"Do you want to taste yourself?" he asked.

"Yes."

He pushed his fingers inside of her mouth and she began to suck and lick them.

"Yeah, get all of your juices off of them," he ordered.

She did as he said and made sure there wasn't any left on his fingers. He slowly pulled them out as he let out a groan in appreciation.

"I want you to accept me," he said.

"Yes," she said with a shaky breath.

She was still in the aftermath of that incredible orgasm and trying her best to stay focused on what he was saying.

"Will you accept me in your mouth?" he asked with a hint of curiosity in his voice.

"In my mouth?" she questioned, confused about what he was asking her.

"Yes. I want you to feel my length and taste me in your mouth."

She shuddered at the image in her head. At first, she wasn't sure what he wanted, but now it was clear. Letting out a shaky breath, she tried to calm herself as she felt damp again.

"Yes," she said.

"Yes, what?" he asked.

"Please, let me take you in my mouth, my lord," she answered.

His clothes ruffled as she imagined he shifted his weight on his feet. She smiled, thinking he must have been adjusting himself. A sound of the zipper slowly being undone echoed in her head. Her body began to shake with anticipation as she had never done such a thing before, but her mouth began to water at all the images of how it would look.

Something gently touched her lips. She slid her tongue out until she made contact with skin. Flicking her tongue, she heard a deep groan come from him. Putting her lips together, she kissed the top of him before taking him into her mouth. Another deep groan left him before he fisted her hair. She began to rock on her knees to move her mouth back and forth over his length. Amara never thought about how big he was until she was using her mouth like a tape measure. He made a few pleasure sounds that were muffled as she pulled away from him.

"Are you enjoying this?" she asked.

"Yes," he answered.

"Then make noises to let me know how I'm doing or else I'm going to think you don't like it," she teased.

Once getting him back inside her mouth and she began working him, she heard his groans get louder, especially when she took him all the way in. He rocked his hips with her. She couldn't help but laugh to herself as she felt him trying to touch the back of her throat. Quickly sucking, she heard him inhale quickly. She loved that she caught him off guard.

Her tongue slowly traced the vein under his need and caused him to rock hard forward into her mouth. She almost gagged, but she calmed her body to accept him. She kept sucking and flicking him with her tongue, feeling he was getting close. Amara would pull away to let him calm before going over the edge of ecstasy as she wanted a little fun and revenge for what he put her through. She figured that would make his orgasm even better than the one she just had minutes ago.

He kept trying to reach his point, but she was able to control him with her mouth. Liam eventually went with the flow with her. She decided after he was a good boy, she would help him reach his release. She quickened her pace and listened to his breathing until he grunted and inhaled quickly. She couldn't do anything as he pressed hard against the back of her throat. When she felt something else hitting the back of her throat, she began to swallow the warm substance. He let out a few quiet grunts as his hips rocked.

After he let out a satisfied sigh, she felt him removing himself. She could imagine he was beyond the ecstasy point and she was glad she was able to pull that off. Before she could say anything, his mouth engulfed hers in a powerful kiss. Goose bumps ran across her skin as she felt how much he appreciated what she did to him.

She exhaled quickly when his mouth finally left hers. Liam helped her off of her knees. In one swift move, he had her on the bed on her back. Her mind couldn't keep up as she felt the bands pull her legs apart. Her urges were an inferno again when she realized she was exposing herself to him.

After feeling his weight on the bed with her, then hovering over her, he removed the blindfold. Her hands pressed against his bare chest, feeling the warmth of his body against hers. She smiled up at him when she saw the haze in his eyes from his orgasm. She could tell it was an incredible one. He stroked her cheek before planting a soft kiss on her lips.

Liam kissed and nibbled down her body until he moved more to the right to flick his tongue on her nipple. She whimpered until he engulfed her nipple in his mouth. The warmness of his mouth sent shivers of excitement throughout her body. He moved over to her other nipple and did the same thing. She arched her back. Her mind had decided that her body now belong to him and do with it as he pleased.

As he continued his oral assault on her body, he gently pushed her hands above her head. The clank of the bands bonding together rang in her ears. When he lifted his head to look at her, her gaze locked with his. Even though she was spread eagle on the bed, she felt covered up with his naked body.

As he pushed inside of her, her insides formed around his length until it was all in. Her body began to quake as he stilled inside of her. She didn't know why he wasn't making love to her until she felt it. He jerked a few times, grunting before bringing his face back to her. Swallowing hard, his cheeks began to redden.

"I'm sorry, all that foreplay caused me to be sensitive," he said.

"Well, it's not like we have a time limit," she teased.

A big smile appeared on his face before leaning down to kiss her. He had the bands release her hands from above her head as he began to thrust into her. She dug her nails into his shoulder blades as his rocking became harder and faster. Amara tried to hold back, but she could feel he was pushing to the point of no return. She held onto him tightly as he pushed as hard as he could into her, finally releasing with her. As they calmed down from hitting that point, he gently kissed her, brushing her hair back. His other arm slithered around her to hold her tight against him. Tears slowly fell from Amara's eyes, not from sadness, but from the strong feelings she had for Liam. She knew where she belonged.

Her hand slid along the scar on his arm and made its way up to touching his beard. Closing her eyes, she took all of him in as it began to become familiar to her. It was just like her dream where they were touching each other. Her body shook as her stomach twisted with nervous excitement bonded together. She couldn't believe she was giving up on her dream companion until she said something that made her realize something.

"Oh, Liam," she gasped when he began to nibble along her jawline.

Realization and recognition dawned. He pulled away when she pushed on his chest. Staring into his eyes, she began to figure out that he was her dream companion. She couldn't believe she never saw it before as she thought for sure he was her enemy. She should have seen it as it was right in front of her. Tears flowed. She couldn't believe how stupid she was. His eyes held concern as he began to stroke her face. She knew he was terrified that maybe he hurt her.

"What's wrong, my firefly?" he asked, voice shaking.

A laugh escaped as she didn't mean it to sound crazy. She couldn't believe that she never recognized the pet name that her dream companion had given to her. She had forgotten that she had shown him the trick she could do before showing Liam. He called her that because she lit up the sky like a firefly when she let the flames engulfed her body. Shaking her head, and covering her eyes, she just couldn't grasp that she had been fighting with someone she had grown up with in her dreams. Feeling his body tense and shaking, she realized she better tell him what was wrong before he shook the answer from her.

"I'm so sorry, Liam," she said.

"Um, for what?"

She uncovered her eyes. "Not seeing what was in front of me," she explained.

He arched his eyebrow, still not sure what she was talking about. She sat up and fell into his arms, holding him tight against her.

"I love you," she whispered in his ear.

***

He tightened his hold on her, closing his eyes. He really enjoyed being with her in harmony instead of fighting. He was happy to finally have her outside the dream world.

"I love you, too, Amara," he said softly.

***

Boris checked to make sure everything was ready. Looking around, he tried to figure out how he was going to get those monsters' attention. Then an idea slowly formed in his mind.

"Let's get wood piled," he ordered.

If that didn't get those beasts' attention, then he didn't know what would. For some reason, those monsters weren't fans of forests being destroyed. An evil smirk appeared on his face as he couldn't wait to get these two.

***

Liam, in his dragon form, walked around, not liking how the area looked. His eyes landed on Amara, in mourning over her destroyed land. He wished that he knew the real reason she tried to escape from him beforehand. If she had told him why she needed to leave, he would have been more willing to compromise and help protect her land. Not keep her prisoner, believing she hated him. It was too late and there wasn't any hope of her area being revived. Letting out a low, rattling growl, he would love to tear those brutal mortals a new one. He would have gone after them, but he needed to be there to support her.

Without warning, she turned into her human form and collapsed on her legs. He quickly went to her and changed as well. She leaned into him as he wrapped his arms around her. She lost all color in her face. He thought for sure she had fallen ill and was going to pass out. The only thing to confirm she wasn't going to faint was when she looked into his eyes. He was glad that she was just really upset about what happened. As he held her, he tried to keep her warm as her body began to shiver. She may have been weak in the legs, but she was determined to stay conscious.

"I can't believe it's all gone," she said softly.

"I'm so sorry. I wished I didn't take you away from here," he tried to console her.

She looked away from him and he panicked. Using his hand, he brought her eyes back to his.

"I'm truly am sorry," he said slowly.

"It was meant to be," she mumbled, looking away.

"What?" he asked.

She looked back into his eyes, searching. "It was meant to be," she repeated.

He wasn't sure what she was talking about. Biting her lower lip, he saw she was still having an internal battle with herself.

"You're the one from my dreams," she said.

"Yes," he said slowly.

"I never got to actually see you," she said quietly.

"Then how did you know it was me?"

She pulled his arm from her. "When I saw your arm with the scar, I knew it was you," she explained.

Tracing the scar with her finger, he could tell she was putting everything together.

"You told me how you got this scar." She looked into his eyes again. "It was when you climbed a tree and fell as a kid," she explained.

"Yes," he said quietly.

"Then when you began to call me Firefly, I really thought you were making fun of me until I realized when you were making love to me, you were really sincere with it. You gave me that nickname after I showed you in my dreams my fire trick. I just figured it was coincidence."

"I would never make fun of you. I just figured you were just angry at me and maybe I grabbed the wrong girl as you didn't act like you did in my dreams," Liam said.

"See, I never saw you in my dreams, but I felt you were there with me in the dark room," she continued.

He tilted his head to the side. "I was able to see you," he said.

"You were?"

"Yeah, I got to watch you grow up into the beautiful woman in front of me."

"I don't understand why I couldn't see you."

"I don't know why either, but I really love the girl in my dreams, who is with me now," he said before planting a soft kiss on her cheek.

As she sighed, she nuzzled into him more. He was glad that things worked out as he almost lost faith in believing she was the same girl from his dreams. Closing his eyes, he wanted to enjoy that moment forever, but the scent of burning wood hit his nose. He looked around, trying to figure out where it was coming from. They weren't close to any villages to be able to smell their fireplaces going.

Slowly standing up, he gently placed Amara on her feet. He held onto her to make sure she wouldn't collapse again, but the smell made him want to go investigate it. He caught the sound of her sniffing the air as well.

"What is that?" she asked.

"No idea why there is wood burning," he answered.

In his gut, he wanted to return to his castle and have his beasts check it out, but in his curious mind, he wanted to check it out himself. It was just an urge he needed to do when something was happening in the woods. He didn't know if it was just their nature to protect the lands or something else. All he knew was that he needed to do something.

"Maybe we should check it out," she implied.

Looking down at her, he was glad she made the decision easier, but there was something still bothering him.

"Okay, let's go in our dragon forms though," he said.

Nodding in agreement, he could tell she was thinking the same thing.

***

Hildebrandt coughed as the smoke from the fire entered his lungs. If his mind wasn't set on patricide, he would have found a way out of that mess. His mind still couldn't understand how his father could treat him so badly. Before he knew it, his father's men strapped him to this pole and started a fire around him. He didn't know why they would do such a thing as he knew he wasn't a warlock of any kind. Shaking his head, he hated how his father just used him for things without any regards that he was a child.

He couldn't wait until he was big and strong so maybe he could knock his father down a few pegs. Of course, he would need to survive this somehow. He tried struggling out of the ropes and chains, but nothing seemed to work. He thought for sure he was a goner as it was becoming harder and harder to breathe.

Thinking he was being delusional, he looked up in the sky and thought he saw two big figures coming toward him. He always tried to act tough in front of his father and his men when they were face to face with beasts, but inside he was terrified. The one creature eyed him suspiciously while the other examined the situation. He thought for sure they would have been burned by the fire, but he kept forgetting that their scales protected them from such harm.

Standing before him were two dragons, one silver and the other red scaled. They stared at him, occasionally looking at each other. Hildebrandt wondered if they were somewhat communicating with each other and what they were saying. The silver-colored dragon rolled its eyes and snorted. He could tell that one seemed annoyed about what the red dragon said.

In an instant, the creature lifted up its talons and hinged it under the chains and ropes before ripping them away like nothing. The red dragon caught Hildebrandt before he fell into the fire with its snout. He wasn't sure how to take that, as no one had ever been nice to him except for his mother, who was long gone. The silver scale dragon stomped on the flames so Hildebrandt could move away from the pole.

Before he could say a word to either of these monsters, men began to yell. Hildebrandt saw the two creatures turn to see they were being surrounded. As they began to flap their wings to get away, chain nets fell on them. Whipping their bodies around to get the nets off, one of them let out a howl of pain. Hildebrandt could see that one of the spears had penetrated through the one creature's leg. The silver scaled dragon growled at the men as the red scaled one continued to howl in pain from the spear.

The men surround them. They struggled as they tried to bring the creatures down to the ground so they could use big wooden stakes. Hildebrandt had never seen the men take down two beasts together and could see it was getting harder for them to do so.

***

Liam knew it was a bad idea, but Amara couldn't let the boy die in the flames. Her compassion saw them both fighting for their lives. Looking over at the boy, he had lost all the color on his face. He soon realized the scrawny brat had no idea what was going to happen and he was really going to be burned alive. Looking over his shoulder, he spotted the leader he had dealt with before. Boris continued to bellow orders, keeping his eyes on Liam.

Liam let out a low, rattling growl before shifting his weight and swiftly moving his tail, swatting the men away like nothing. Letting out a raspy laugh, Liam enjoyed it as he shifted his weight toward his right and swiped his tail at the men near Amara. She looked at him like he lost his mind. He smiled as he slowly rolled to his side and pulled her toward him. Before she knew what was happening, he rolled with her safely in his wings wrapped around her. The men yelled as some of them almost got flattened by Liam's stunt.

***

Amara saw the men trying to stop them as she began to get use to this and let out raspy laughs as well. Before long, she spotted large, wooden spikes to prevent them from rolling to safety and they couldn't fly because of the nets. She thought for sure they were out of options until Liam sent a message to her in her mind. She let a small smile sneak up on her face.

Before those men could do anything to stop them, she set them on fire. As they continued to roll toward the spikes, she saw the men getting antsy as they tried to block them from escaping. They smashed right through the spikes as debris and flame shoot away from it, causing the men to leap out of the way.

The flames consuming their bodies soon broke the ropes and melted the chains as the nets disintegrate off their bodies. Before those men could catch up to them, Amara and Liam quickly got on their feet and flap their wings to fly away. As the men's yells echoed up to them, Amara let out a raspy laugh, enjoying the pounding of her heart. They soon disappeared into the clouds as Amara did barrel rolls next to Liam.

***

Liam arched his eyebrow as he looked at Amara. He could see she was enjoying that thrill, but he panicked when they were almost captured. As he continued to watch her roll and swoop around, he let a smile appear on his face. He realized it was a thrilling ride and began to roll and swoop around with her.

Maybe it wasn't as bad as I thought...

Chapter Nine

Lord Kane watched as his men got their gear and armor ready. He wanted to make sure he had enough men just in case there were more dragons at the castle that they were attacking.

"Remember, the female is off limits and should not be harmed," he ordered

"Ay, sir," his men shouted in unison.

Looking over, he spotted Nikolai leaning against the doorway with his arms crossed and Nadia standing behind him. He knew Nikolai was angry he couldn't go with them, but he didn't want to take a chance with his life yet. He was a strong warrior, but still young minded in fighting. Lord Kane wanted him to stay here in case none of them, especially himself, didn't return. He needed another alpha male to be king and take care of the tribe. With Nadia's help, he could tell that Nikolai would do a good job and avenge his death if it happened.

Looking back at his men, he knew soon they would either succeed or fail in their mission. His eyes traveled up to the big hall's high ceiling, hoping that they would succeed so his tribe would survive.

Please have mercy on us and let us win…

***

Liam stirred in bed with his eyes closed. He couldn't wipe the big smile off his face, even if he wanted to. After their incredible escape, they came back here and continued to laugh their asses off in their human forms. Before long, Amara was on him as if she needed him to live. He found her aggressiveness thrilling as he didn't deny her of anything.

Rolling over, he got a face full of her hair. Inhaling slowly before letting out a satisfied sigh. They mated the whole night in different positions, but she was the first to wither, sometime in the morning. He rested his arm around her as he enjoyed having her there instead of just in his dreams.

She began to stir before sitting up. Rolling onto his back, he watched her look over her shoulder. The morning sun made her skin and hair even more radiant, as if she had an aura around her. He quickly pinched himself to make sure he wasn't dreaming and she was really there. Exhaling slowly, he was glad she was really here. His chest tightened a bit when he thought it was all a dream, but loosened when he realized it all really happened.

"What are you looking at?" she asked.

"The most beautiful thing in the world," he answered.

She let out a laugh with a big smile. He loved hearing that sound from her and seeing that she was happy with him. He never wanted to go back to what they were before when he brought her to be with him. He didn't like seeing the unhappiness in her eyes as she would fight with him tooth and nail. He had never met anyone like her before, especially when she didn't recognize him. He was happy it finally all worked out.

Before she decided to get up, he quickly wrapped her up in his arms and rolled her on top of him so he could feel her close to him. She tried to squirm and fight her way out of his hold, but eventually she gave up and nuzzled against him. He could get used to such a life.

***

Boris and his men stared up at the castle before them from the woods. He smiled wickedly as he knew they had found the monsters' nest. Examining the place, he didn't see any guards or defense anywhere. He began to wonder if it was just the creatures or if there was something else. He had to make a decision before it got dark. Looking back at his men, he knew what they were going to do.

***

Lord Kane and his army surveyed the castle from the cliffs. He quickly examined it and had a scout check it out before they attacked. He didn't want to get caught off guard. Sniffing the air, he knew the female was close. He hoped she hadn't mated with the male yet so she could take his seed and help produce more ice dragons. He didn't need an offspring from the male in his tribe. He only wanted the strong and not some full-blooded, weak fire dragon. His eyes fell on a man, dressed in armor, climbing up the cliff before kneeling before him. A falcon landed on his shoulder as he placed his arm across his chest and lowered his head.

"My Lord, I had not spotted any defenses or guards. We may be able to take the castle and get the female without much causality," he explained.

"Good," Lord Kane said.

Looking down at the castle again, he knew they should attack soon in order to maintain the element of surprise. He couldn't wait to get the female back to their home, so they could expand the tribe. It had been a while since he was with his mate, and had been the love of his life. He chuckled, as he knew this female would just be a producer, nothing more. No one could replace his mate, not even a female with so much to offer. Licking his lips, he couldn't wait to spill the blood of the male dragon.

**

Even though, Liam was enjoying Amara's company, he felt uneasy for some odd reason. He could tell she was feeling the same thing. Occasionally, he looked out the window, but he couldn't see anything. He felt forces nearby, but nothing appeared in the area. Sniffing the air, he smelled something. Amara did as well.

He was about to send out some of his minions to check it out, but all of a sudden, the castle rumbled. Liam grabbed hold of Amara before she fell. She looked up at him, furrowing her brow. He didn't have a clue what could have caused the castle to quake like that. He was going to help relieve the stress, but the castle rumbled again.

Before he got Amara squarely on her feet, he ran toward a window. Looking out, he spotted catapults, shooting boulders at the castle. He let out a low, rattling growl when he saw Boris and his men. He was about to jump out the window to take care of them, but something caught his attention. He turned to look at Amara.

"Liam! Ice Dragons!" she shouted, pointing into the sky.

He ran over to the window and spotted a dozen or more ice dragons descending from the cliffs, some in their dragon forms and others in their human forms dressed in armor. He couldn't believe their luck as he thought maybe they wouldn't have to deal with such an ordeal today.

"Hagar!" he shouted.

A big, hairy beast showed up in front of him. Liam looked at the commander of his minions and knew they would have to battle to go back to a happy life.

"Get the others ready. We're going to war," Liam ordered.

The beast snorted before leaving to fetch his comrades. Liam turned to look at Amara. He didn't want her to fight, but he knew they needed all the help they could get. He was worried she may be harmed or taken away. He knew the ice dragons were here for her.

"Come on," he said softly, his hand out toward her.

Without hesitation, she grabbed hold of his hand. Tugging her along, he knew they had to reach a better vantage point before attacking. Usually, he wouldn't go so fast, but they didn't really have the time. He was glad that she was able to keep up with him.

Hurrying down into the armory, he knew they would need weapons. He grabbed a Spartan helmet and turned around to put it on her. Her hands rested on top of his as he fitted the helmet on her head. He stilled as her fearful ruby red eyes stared into his. His own right hand trembled in terror. He had never been so scared, but knowing what was at stake made panic.

"Hey, we're going to be okay," she said softly.

Looking back into her eyes, he could tell she was telling the truth. Before he could stop himself, his lips were on hers. He pressed hard against them for fear it would be their last kiss.

Pulling away, he saw she was still in a haze. He had to hold her steady as she almost fell forward. Once she was steady, he handed her a sword. She admired it for a moment as it glistened in the light. Her eyes returned to his.

"Ready?" he asked.

She nodded. "Ready."

The butterflies in his stomach were back and his heart pounded harder. He wasn't even sure if he was ready. He admired her for a few minutes more, just in case they didn't make it out alive.

Here's to hope…

***

"Fire!" Boris yelled.

More boulders shot through the air and hit the castle. Boris smiled and saw how the castle was slowly deteriorating from their attacks. Before they could continue, Boris put his hand up to stop the men from firing and yelling. Squinting his eyes, he tried to listen to a sound that caught his attention. His eyes soon land on something climbing down the castle wall.

As it started as one, it multiplied to more big hairy creatures. He grated his teeth in anticipation before raising his arm with a sword in his hand.

"Attack!" he yelled the order.

His men yelled a battle cry before charging toward the creatures. The creatures let out roars and howls, running on all four. The beasts and the men clashed, the clang of metal and tear of flesh echoed through the battlefield.

Boris easily took down some of the creatures with his battle axe before looking up at the castle. He didn't want to mess with such pesky monsters. He'd come for bigger game. Glancing over his shoulder, it looked like his men were doing a good job of pushing the hairy beasts back. But in an instant that changed as a silver scaled dragon swept in, knocking all his men down. The monster twisted and turned until it was in human form on the ground. Boris spotted him looking straight at him before turning to run toward the woods. Boris followed suit as he was determined to at least kill the male dragon.

Once he entered the woods, he looked around cautiously. He didn't want the monster to get the upper hand. He stilled as his eyes widened when he heard someone behind him. He turned around, ready to wield his ax but stopped.

"You?" he questioned, confusion in his voice.

Before he could do anything, he let out a yell as something attacked him.

***

Some of the ice dragons in their human forms made it into the castle. As they spread out, they searched the castle. As a few entered one room, Amara came around a wall and started to fight with them with her sword and shield. They hesitated with their attacks as they didn't want to be punished for going against Kane's orders, but at the same time they were trying to defend themselves. Blood sprayed all over her as she sliced through her enemies' flesh.

She kept going as she knew they would keep coming after her. She wasn't going to let them win without a fight. Letting out her own battle cry, lifting up her sword, she watched as all of them stilled. She could tell they were terrified of her, but they still had their orders. She just wished they would fight her instead of holding back as it made it too easy.

Typical chivalric males…

***

Liam kept swinging a battle ax he found as he and his beasts kept pushing the men back. When he heard a roar, he stopped and looked up at the castle. He spotted a dragon with black and red scales. His eyes widened as he realized that must be the alpha dragon. The alpha head butted the wall of the castle before climbing into it. Liam left the battle to his beasts and ran toward the castle. He needed to save Amara before she got captured.

Smashing through the heavy wooden door, he looked around and saw bodies everywhere. He let a smile appear on his face, liking how Amara took care of the ice dragons. Before he could enjoy the moment, he heard her scream. He raced up the stairs so quickly, he wasn't sure if his feet touched any of them.

Liam almost slid past a doorway. He cautiously walked in, letting out a low, rattling growl toward the intruder. He had Amara pressed against the wall, pinned with his talons. The creature turned its head and glared at Liam. Liam's eyes darkened as he snarled. He was not about to let that monster take Amara away from him after all he had gone through to get her.

Liam heard something that made him freeze in his spot. His jaw slowly dropped open as his body went cold. Dropping the battle ax, his grip shook so badly that his fingers let it go. He couldn't believe what he heard that made his blood run cold.

"She's mine," the ice dragon rasped.

Liam couldn't believe he was face to face with the beast that haunted his nightmares. He thought he would never meet him, but standing before him was the alpha dragon that claimed Amara as his own.

"Liam," Amara cried out.

Liam looked over at Amara. She was terrified. Shaking his head, he got his mind focused on what he needed to do. He growled as his eyes flashed brighter. He wanted the alpha dragon to know Amara didn't belong to anyone but him. He could tell his disobedience was pissing off the alpha as it let out roar before letting Amara go where she collapsed to the ground. The dragon charged at Liam. Before the beast could snap his teeth on Liam like a bear trap, Liam quickly bent over to pick up the ax and rolled under the creature.

The alpha spun around, trying to get at Liam who was still under him. As the creature moved, Liam sliced at the dragon's legs, causing it to howl in pain. Before Liam could slice at the alpha's last leg, he snapped his jaw on Liam's ankle and threw him across the room. Liam's back hit the solid stone wall before he fell face first to the floor. The ax clanked off the ground a few times. Liam groaned as he tried to get up. He looked up when he felt the ground shake from the creature bound toward him.

Before Liam could defend himself, the alpha shoved his head under him and pushed both of them out of the castle. As they fell, Liam punched the alpha a few times as he snapped his jaw at him. Liam hit the ground first and rolled out of the way before the beast slammed his feet on him.

Laying on his stomach and elbow, Liam glared at Lord Kane. Kane snarled. Liam could see how much the other dragon wanted to kill him. Scrambling from the ground, he quickly turned into his dragon form and attacked the alpha. They rolled around on the ground, growling and trying to claw each other. Lord Kane threw Liam off and was about to bring his talons down on him, but he was quickly subdued by Liam's minions.

Liam knew he needed to end it before this alpha succeeded in killing him. Getting to his feet slowly, groaning from his injuries, Liam made his way toward the mountain side. He looked up to see if this would work as he listened to the beasts battle it out with the alpha behind him.

Looking over his shoulder, he spotted the alpha whipping the beasts off of him. The alpha looked right at Liam, but Liam returned his attention to the vertical stone wall he would have to climb. Without hesitation, he dug in the first set of claws and started the long climb. He listened to the alpha charge toward him before he climbed after Liam. Liam was surprised the creature followed his lead when it could easily fly up the mountain. He hoped the alpha kept following him.

Liam was going to fly up the rest of the way, but when he tried flapping his wings, his left one shook from severe pain. He didn't realize how much damage the alpha had done. More determined, he focused on climbing faster than the alpha so his plan would work.

Finally, reaching the top, Liam collapsed on the ground to try to catch his breathe. Before he could get situated, he turned over in time to have the alpha pin him down. Lord Kane growled in his face. Liam was doomed.

"Fool," Lord Kane rasped out the word.

Liam tried to struggle out of his grip, but Kane slammed him down on the ground and made his head spin from the impact. He had to shake his head to get the blurriness from his eyes. Kane's face was only inches away. Letting out more low, rattling growls, Liam continued to struggle, but stopped when Lord Kane let out raspy laughs.

Did you really think you could have her? Lord Kane sent the message in Liam's mind.

Liam tried getting out from being pinned down, but Lord Kane slammed his talons down on him and enclosed Liam's throat in them.

Did you really think you could have defeated me, boy? Lord Kane said in Liam's mind.

"No…but she could," Liam rasped out slowly.

***

Before Lord Kane knew what happened, he turned to look over his shoulder and watched as four sets of talons came at him from a red scaled dragon. Kane crumbled near the edge of a cliff and looked up in time to watch Amara lift up her front talons and claw right through his wings when he tried to open them to fly away. She then shoved him in the chest with the top of her head, causing him to fall backward. Looking over the edge, she watched as Lord Kane fell until he disappeared into the forest below. She listened to see if he was still alive, but the only sound that caught her attention was Liam coughing.

Quickly going to him, she examined him. He nudged under her jaw to let her know he was okay. She couldn't help but smile. His plan worked. He was going to be the distraction so she could get the jump on the alpha and take care of him. She almost missed her queue when more of the ice dragons tried attacking her. Lucky for Liam, she made it in time before that alpha killed him.

Liam looked up into the sky as she followed his gaze. They watched as the ice dragons retreated. She looked over the edge when she heard the beasts howling and saw those men retreating as well. Her eyes returned to Liam as she sent him the message that the men were leaving as well.

Liam slowly turned back into his human form and collapsed on his back with his arm over his eyes. She changed as well and rushed to him, thinking he was seriously injured, but she spotted him peeking from under his arm and smiling at her.

"I knew you weren't a damsel in distressed," he teased.

Amara couldn't help but laugh, and soon he joined her. She was glad he knew she could take care of herself without a male's help. Before he knew it, she planted her lips on his and his arms wrapped around her. She melted against his body. She never wanted to leave his side ever again.

***

As the men grumbled and groaned from their injuries, they caught the sound of alarm.

"Help!"

Running toward the yell, they all stop a few feet from Boris, on the ground, choking on his own blood. Kneeling next to him was Hildebrandt with all the color gone from his face.

"Please, help," Hildebrandt cried out.

The second in command rushed over and pushed Hildebrandt out of the way. Examining Boris, he spotted what looked like some damage to his throat. If he didn't know any better, he would say it was a dragon's bite.

He looked over his shoulder at Hildebrandt. "What happened?" he asked.

"It was the silver scale dragon. He attacked him," Hildebrandt explained.

Looking back at Boris, he continued to cough and choke. He lifted up his shaky arm and pointed up toward the sky. The second-in-command watched as Boris tried to say something. Blood splattered his lips.

"No…Dragon," Boris choked out.

Before he could get a complete explanation of what he was trying to say, Boris let out one last breathe. The second-in-command tried to wake him, but realized he was gone. Closing his eyes, he looked over his shoulder.

"Take him with us," he ordered.

A few men bent down and picked up Boris to carry him away. The second in command stood next to Hildebrandt as he stared where his father was. Placing a hand on his shoulder, he tried to console the boy.

"Sorry for ye loss," he said.

Hildebrandt looked over at the second in command, before he joined the rest of the group of men. They continued their journey home in silence in respect to Boris.

***

The ice dragons grumbled in the hall, wondering what they would do without their alpha. Without warning, the big wooden doors swung open revealing a figured that was slowly healing. Not a single one could muster a sound or a word as Lord Kane made his way to his throne.

"Thanks for leaving me behind," he grated.

They continued to stare at him in awe. Sitting on the throne, he closed his eyes for a second to let the pain pass. He opened them again to look at his tribe.

"We'll have to find another female and forget that one back at the castle," he ordered

His tribe grumbled amongst themselves as Lord Kane stroked his beard. Something else was troubling him. Looking into the darkness, he watched as Vladimir's eyes glowed like two hot coals. Kane could feel the trouble brewing inside of him.

What to do with him?

***

As Boris lay on a wooden table, the second-in-command rubbed his beard. Something troubled him about Boris' death. Slowly making his way toward Boris, he gradually removed the tarp covering up the body. Leaning closer, he examined the injury again. He felt a chill ran through his veins as his eyes widened.

"That's not a dragon's bite," he whispered to himself.

Rushing out of the room and out the door, he looked around wildly. Some of the men stood next to him.

"What's going on?" one asked.

"Where's Hildebrandt?" he asked.

They all looked around, not seeing him anywhere. One looked back at the second in command.

"Why?" another asked.

"We have been fooled," he answered.

The second-in-command felt eyes on him. The other men have no idea what he was talking about, but it was as clear as day to him. He recalled how Boris pointed, he soon realized that Boris was pointing at Hildebrandt and trying to explain that it wasn't a dragon that killed him, but his son. Unfortunately, the second-in-command couldn't put that together as he felt the loss of their leader.

It made perfect sense as he thought he saw the silver scaled dragon fighting another dragon so he wasn't sure when that dragon could have killed Boris. His body began to shake in terror. It wasn't a beast that he was afraid of, but a boy.

***

Hildebrandt reached the top of a mountain and stared at the horizon. He let a wicked smile spread across his face. He couldn't believe he made those fools believe that a dragon killed his father.

Flashing back, he recalled how he met his father in the woods when he thought he was chasing that silver scaled dragon. His father turned around and was about to bring his battle ax down on him, but stopped. Before his father knew what was happening, Hildebrandt used a special tool to make it look like a dragon attacked his father. Before calling for help, he made sure to hide the tool before the other men discovered it. Of course, the second-in-command was sniffing too closely so he knew he needed to move on from the group.

Looking down at the tool in his hand, his smile grew bigger. This tool had done so much for him. Walking over to a large crack in the stone, he dropped it down it. He listened as it clanked and hit off the sides before he couldn't hear it anymore. Walking to the edge, he looked out and spotted a town a few miles away as their lighted windows gave way to where they were located. Gradually climbing down, he knew he had a new opportunity and was able to get rid of the bastard of a father as well.

Life couldn't get any better than this.

About the Author

Born in Denver, Colorado, Dawn L. Lubertowicz spent most of her formative years traveling the world with her family, during which time she learnt about many different cultures. In 1990 the Persian Gulf War brought all of that to an end and she moved back to the United States with her mother and her older sister. Finally, she married and settled in the small town of Tunkhannock with her husband, Jason, and their 'furry children', Zack, Storm, Clark, and Fudge.

Dawn injects a sense of humor and depth to each of her characters, giving them each an individual dynamic that makes them both interesting and engaging Her witty personality and endless imagination allow her to weave tales that are intriguing and thoroughly entertaining, and will keep you reading to the end. As you fall in love with her characters you will feel their pain, happiness, sadness, and humor, as you live their story with them.

Previously, Dawn went to college and graduated with a Bachelor's Degree in Psychology, minored in Criminal Justice, and has a certificate in Forensic Science.